Sword Without Shield

a Fluffy Mystery

K.A. Bachus

For Buster, Kelly, Tippy, Gus, Corky, Barney, Sherlock, Winston, Saxon, Jethro, Marigold, Archie, Faith, Agatha, Joy, Badger, Sophie, Phryne, Donovan, and above all, George—with gratitude for all the times we've had together—especially the difficult ones.

PROLOGUE

He looked again, hard. Was it him? They were both older, with less hair, more weight. If it *was* him. His Honor, Mayor Bobby Greene hoped he was wrong. It had to be a memory, a stray resemblance. The universe could not, must not, land that man here.

The excitement caused by the news that they finally found a contractor to run the town's airport made this meet and greet gathering of the Morgan City Council a festive occasion. Somebody brought beer. One of the wives laid out a pan of hot wings on a long table set up against one wall of the hangar where they met. Another woman provided potato salad, chips, salsa, and a creamy ranch dip. Bobby's third wife put a Pyrex bowl on the table, opened a tin of mixed nuts, and dumped in the contents. With a scowl. Always with a scowl. Only the grandkids kept them from killing each other.

The president of the council stood on a large toolbox as a stiff wind blew fallen maple leaves through the open hangar doors. He formally introduced the newcomer. Bobby already knew the name; he was mayor for God's sake, and had been present when the lease was signed. It wasn't like the name Lewis Caslander was common. It should have twigged his memory immediately. Why did it take seeing the man to bring his mind back to Thailand all those years ago?

Bobby gazed at his pride and joy, *Marybelle*, the Cessna 140 sheltered a few feet away. He loved that airplane and hated the memories of that other time now resurrected by the intruder approaching to shake his hand.

"Long time no see," said Lew, hand extended.

Bobby would rather grasp a jungle viper, but he had responsibilities.

And maybe Lew would keep his damned mouth shut.

1

Indian Island, Maine
July, 2000

"Tell me again why I am here?" Christine tore her eyes from the corpse to look at the man who had called her. She knew her presence made the forensics team unhappy. If it were her case, she would be.

"We need one of ours who knows what they're looking at, just in case one of ours did this. Or didn't."

Or didn't, but they want to pin it on him. She nodded and mentally completed the thought for the tall businessman, a Penobscot tribal elder who had brought her here. His manner suggested so many things: education, command, and maybe arrogance—or was it just confidence? George James was a leader, for sure. The kind you want in difficult situations. He expected her to fall in line. Christine obliged reluctantly.

She needed to make it fast. The gatekeeper on the pathology team who let them in would be overruled any minute by the forensic team leader. She took in the scene.

A struggle. The man had fought his losing battle strenuously, using every liftable piece of furniture in the room. Chairs and a coffee table showed the same slash wounds as the body. A decorated sword, probably Asian, lay bloody on the floor. An empty set of brackets in a wall display of similar weapons glistened with smeared blood.

"Are there any wounds other than the sword cuts?" she asked the increasingly unfriendly team leader.

"A bullet," he said with a nod. "It wasn't lethal."

True, it wasn't, or he would not have been able to reach the sword on the wall.

"But it weakened him?" said Christine.

"Yes. Nicked the vena cava, maybe. Won't know until they open him. Some of the blood might be the murderer's. Again, we won't know until we test. Either way, there's enough DNA in here after a struggle like this."

Unspoken: *Please stop adding yours to the mix.*

"Okay," she said to the elder who had pulled the strings to get her in here. "We should leave now."

The pathologist smiled.

...

"Listen, George, I'm not sure I can help you," said Christine, her hand on the door handle of her black 4X4 Jeep. "This is what I would call a full-time case and I don't have it—time, I mean." She tried to soften her refusal with a smile.

He loomed over her, scowling down his long nose into her eyes. He wore an expensive suit and even pricier black shoes. His shirt and tie completed the required uniform for an educated businessman in DownEast Maine. Only the ponytail at the nape of his neck indicated his Native heritage.

"We'll pay your going rate, Christine—your full-time rate."

She could tell he didn't think she had anything else to do. They had met the month before when she first arrived in Bangor from Vermont. He was now only marginally less dismissive of her than he was then—now that he needed her. To be fair, it would be remarkable for any ex-cop from out of state to set up shop as an investigator and develop a client list within a month, so he might be justified in assuming she wasn't busy. But George didn't know about all the other irons heating up in her fire, and she couldn't tell him.

"There are plenty of private detectives in this state, George. I can get you a contact list." She squeezed the door handle under her fingers, wishing it wasn't locked, wanting to get busy erasing the scene in that house from her mind. They stood in the driveway of a quiet two-story, cape-style home on a residential street filled with the silence of spent horror. Her career as a state trooper had shown her worse, but she was reluctant to start her new life this way.

She recognized the quiet Penobscot word he spoke, though he pronounced it differently. An expression of skepticism, just this side of scorn, a gentler form of bullshit, one that she had heard her father say so often. She realized most of her Algonquian language consisted of such words. It was only as an adult that she felt the loss of fluency in her Abenaki heritage and regretted it. Her parents had been too busy working for survival during the short intervals when they managed to pull her and her brother out of foster care. They tried. She understood much of the ancient language she connected with love, but never managed the soft fluency she always wanted.

This man had plenty of fluency, but in that one word, she heard a challenge. She must respond.

"Why, exactly, are you concerned, George? A white guy dies in an Indian woman's house. So what? She couldn't have killed him with a sword. She's barely five feet tall." Christine glanced at the modest house standing in a trim garden amid tall, straight trunks that formed an evergreen canopy seventy feet above. A placid channel of the Penobscot River flowed slowly behind the house while a clump of people patted the back of the diminutive, weeping discoverer of the body.

George converted his request into a demand with four words.

"She has a son."

2

Fluffy glanced at Christine as she turned the car toward the bridge into Old Town. "Where should I start?" she said. She often made such noises and he understood much about her moods because of them. She was uncertain today. He felt it in the sliding sounds of her slow noises. She had tucked up her dark brown hair under a ball cap, but long wisps escaped down the back of her neck and over her ears. The air from the air conditioner made them float at times.

Fluffy sat upright in his elevated doggy car seat, large ears erect, nose pointing forward, eyes watching the road with careful interest. He carried his ten-pound, sleek brown and white body with the assurance of the apex predator he knew he was. The beloved human beside him continued to make noises, long ones with music and shorter ones like footsteps. He found the sound comforting as he watched for threats along their way.

"I'm not even unpacked yet." She caught a wisp of hair flying across her right cheek and tucked it back behind the ear. "The office isn't ready. They installed the T-1 line Justin ordered for me only yesterday. I can't believe I let Frank Cardova talk me into this. What was I thinking? Did I even want to go private and move to Maine? I don't miss being a trooper, but I hated leaving Vermont. I told Frank...."

Fluffy recognized that sound, heard the discomfort in her words, and was not surprised. The word frank evoked memory of a scent attached to an aged, round man without fur where humans usually wore it. The man locked Fluffy in an attic—not without a fight, mind. Fluffy paid him back by eliminating the laces of his shoe.

When she paused between noises, he growled to show her he agreed The Frank was bad news.

"I guess I should ask Justin," said Christine. "If I were still working for the state, I would check NCIC. If I know our new employers, Fluffbutt, Justin's got more dirt than even the National Crime Information Center."

Fluffbutt was a term of respect. It always came with a confidential tone, and sometimes a belly rub. The word justin referred to two machines, one with a bell, and the other with a big lighted screen that drew her attention at inconvenient times, like right at Fluffy's suppertime.

She stopped the car because the car in front of them made them stay. This often happened. Another inexplicable human habit. Christine glanced at the closed notebook on the seat under Fluffy's elevated perch and mumbled, "I need to remember the names George gave me." She opened the book and pulled it toward her, still mumbling, "Dead guy is Lewis Caslander and the girlfriend is Mary Catherine Rogers. Her kid's name is Joseph Stinson. At least I have a starting point."

Fluffy didn't know why she liked to play with the notebook, but he approved of her tendency to chew on a pen in between scribbles. Her teeth barely made a mark though. A deficiency of the species. She closed the book with a snap when loud noises behind them made her look up and drive forward.

As Christine drove the Jeep around the back of their new house, Fluffy's tail wagged. Sometimes, his tail was the first part of him to recognize a happiness. If he was in the habit of personal reflection, which he wasn't, he would have realized the new place held a lot of plusses for him, not the least being all of the smells here were their own. Nobody else shared the space. His supper dish was here. Above all, she was happy here. He felt it in the way she laughed at The Ringing Justin, in the speed with which she climbed the stairs—only one set of these instead of three—and in the music that came out of another machine. Sometimes she danced.

She parked the car under the upper back half of the house, behind the downstairs part that held her office. The overhanging second floor contained their apartment and created shelter for two cars. When Christine opened the back door to the staircase, Fluffy lunged up the first few steps, heading for his supper bowl, but she called him back down.

"Not yet, Fluff. Work to do." She opened the interior door to her glass-fronted office. Cheap shades obscured empty parking spots in front of the building.

To Fluffy's intense disappointment, she picked up The Ringing Justin and turned on The Flashing Justin. He sighed, took a drink from his water bowl in the corner, and jumped into the easy chair next to it. He curled up for a snooze.

"Justin, I have my first case. I need information. How do you want me to search these names?" There was a pause as Fluffy's eyes closed. They opened again at the end of her next sentence.

"I'd like to have the information before I call Frank."

Fluffy growled.

3

Christine took an inch-thick pile of paper from the fancy combo fax/printer Frank had sent her. The department never had anything that sleek. She'd expected a car-sized finicky behemoth that drank expensive toner and always made a mess. This one required long cartridges in individual colors. Easier and neater to use. But still expensive.

She used a three-hole punch on slim stacks and filled a black binder with the printed sheets. Justin also sent the information to her email account. Frank had given her a notebook computer she could use to read instead of using paper, but she hadn't figured out how to use it yet. The world did not end with the turn of the century six months before; the computers weathered Y2K without disaster, but the speed of technological change meant Christine spent more and more time puzzling over the new tools meant to save time.

This, her first solo case, did not give her the luxury of time to fiddle with machines. When the massive copier she expected turned out to be an efficient compact, she used the space for a convenient countertop to hold older twentieth-century technology—a drip coffee maker and a hot plate. A large pot of Labrador tea, the beverage her family called Indian tea, simmered on the hot plate. She dipped in a clean mug, dried the outside, dislodged Fluffy from the easy chair, and settled down with him in her lap. Tea, a notebook, and a highlighter became the first tools of her new professional life.

This is not so bad. Ordinary crime of passion, no doubt. No spooks involved.

She opened the notebook. Air America? Wasn't that a CIA operation? *Shit.* The victim was a spook. Why was she not surprised? That funny old man, Frank, entered her world last year, bringing his skulking universe with him. It was going to be devilishly hard to find info... wait....

"Frank brought me Justin, too," she said aloud. She leafed through the next five pages. No shortage of information here. "Thank you, Justin!" She took a sip of tea and began reading.

Fluffy picked up and tilted his head at the sound of the name, pointing his nose at the computer screen on her desk. Christine dived into the world of the previous generation, where Lewis Caslander flew helicopters from a base in Thailand during the Vietnam War. He patrolled over the Laotian border in support of clandestine operations, receiving several classified commendations, two of which were for valor under fire.

So, he was one of those flying spooks, like a guy she met in Frank's orbit, a particularly nasty piece of work with eyes like melting chocolate. Eyes that wandered, and a look that attracted any woman alive to the male mystique. There was a thought. Caslander did not appear particularly attractive in death, but his murder occurred in his girlfriend's house. Could it be the usual crime of passion over a love affair?

Oh, please let it be that.

But then again, that would bring it too close to George's people. She remembered the weeping woman surrounded by friends in front of her home and shook herself. The best way to screw this up was to care about the outcome. Compassion could only handicap discernment. Besides, the private investigator thing was supposed to be a simple matter of tracking wayward spouses in preparation for divorce. Having a grisly murder to puzzle over was not in the plan. It would interfere with her true purpose in moving to Maine.

Time to call Frank. She picked up the secure phone he had installed on the little table next to her, dialed, and remembered to squeeze the handset when he answered.

"Frank, I have my first case, and I...."

She noticed Fluffy curl a lip at the sound of the name, showing one canine tooth.

"Oh, then Justin has told you about it," she said. "I printed the information he sent me and I'm reading it now. The victim was Air America."

"Long time ago, my dear," said Frank. "Don't forget to put all that paper in your safe, won't you? Are you suspecting an intelligence angle?"

"Why not? He was one of your lot."

"Again, long ago. What else have you got?"

She grimaced, then steeled herself into objectivity. Even if Caslander had died in some kind of spook vengeance event, how would she prove it? The authorities would still pin it on somebody from the Penobscot reservation.

"I've been told his girlfriend's son didn't like him. And that's about it, so far. Maybe there's more to it, but I called because this case is going to make me busier than I expected. I don't think I can spare the time to meet with the instructor you're sending."

"He'll collect you at seven tomorrow. You're an organized person, Christine. You need this. You agreed to it. Cody's doing well, by the way, and sends his love."

"You mean my son mentioned in a random way that he has a mother, Frank. He never went so far as to say those things. Tell him I'll see him when I see him. He'll like that."

Frank chuckled. "The real name of the guy you're meeting tomorrow is Damon Kowalski. Game name is Paul Mathews. You have the authentication instructions. Don't let the last time you met him put you off. He's the real deal now."

"Wait. What? I met him?"

"Stick to protocol, Christine. Love, Frank." There was a smacking sound of a kiss and then dial tone.

She put the phone away and gently put Fluffy back on the chair as she stood up.

"I'll ask Justin who this Damon Kowalski is, Fluffbutt. Then it'll be suppertime."

She gave up on Justin answering her question after an hour, during which time, she became a mini-expert on the subject of Lewis Caslander, and Fluffy worried about starvation.

4

Fluffy sat at the bottom of his favorite over-the-shoulder carrier. Christine's steps down the narrow staircase at the back of the apartment bounced him against her hip in a way that comforted. He knew The Frank disliked him as much as he returned the favor, but as long as he was with Christine, he could put up with it.

He must put up with it. He must protect her.

The Frank had come by the apartment above the office last night. Fluffy gave him what for, only settling into a lip-curling snarl when Christine held him in her arms while they argued. At least he assumed it was an argument because it was loud and long and sometimes about him.

"You can't bring the dog, Christine," said The Frank. "You're going for training. Part of that is to learn to be inconspicuous. The dog is conspicuous." He pointed at Fluffy.

Fluffy bared all his front teeth.

"He's going with. I can't leave him alone in a new place. When I have to be inconspicuous, I'll work it out. For now, the stress is too much for him."

The Frank's bulgy eyes looked at the ceiling and he sighed. "Can you hide him somehow?"

Christine pointed to Fluffy's favorite carrier on the kitchen table.

"It looks like a purse, Frank. See the mesh at the top? Fluffy can see out but people can't see in."

"Until he starts howling...."

"He doesn't howl when he's with me."

Fluffy quietly showed The Frank his fearsome teeth again, hoping he got the point. His point—that The Frank was not welcome here. Fluffy knew it worked when the smell of tension subsided.

"Okay," said The Frank. "We'll consider the carrier and its contents as part of your authentication. I need to know exactly what you'll be wearing, and you should have a book in your hand. What book will you be carrying?"

She held up a copy of *The Spy Who Came in from the Cold*, by John Le Carré.

"Oh for heavens...."

"It's my new reading program, Frank. I find it instructive."

"Fine. You know all the recognition signs. If they are all there and you recognize him and it unsettles you, then that's the guy. Get in the truck with him and he'll take it from there. I have a flight to catch. Use the other number I gave you if you need anything in the next few hours. I'll be available again once I land."

Fluffy bit The Frank's ankle on his way out. He was pleased by the familiar words, "damn dog."

The next morning, Fluffy and Christine reached the downstairs back door with two minutes to spare and watched through the glass panel.

"Blue pickup," murmured Christine as it drove up next to her car. The driver's window came down and a hairy arm used a cloth to wipe the side mirror.

"Yellow rag," said Christine.

The left blinker turned on, then stopped. Twice.

"Blinker."

The man leaned through the open window to look at the back of his truck. He had long dark hair liberally mixed with grey. Fluffy had no opinion of him until he felt Christine's body stiffen and heard her say another word he recognized.

"Shit."

She hesitated and stood a little taller, right arm protectively wrapped around the carrier. "It's you and me, Fluffy. Frank will answer for this." Then, she stepped forward.

Fluffy didn't need sound to know about the emotional state within the single-cab truck. He smelled all of it, but mostly anger, dismay, embarrassment, fear, disdain, disgust. The humans sat rigidly eyes front while the man turned the wheel this way and that. Fluffy would have considered him an enemy except that he was the one who smelled like fear, dismay, and embarrassment. It was Fluffy's beloved Christine who held powerful anger at the end of a breaking leash.

He wondered if he would be allowed to participate in whatever it was she was going to do to this man.

5

Paul's eyes concentrated on the road, his mind on his passenger. She was there, in the truck, next to him, stony face forward, an angry goddess. Who could blame her? How to start? From all the way back to last year or from six months ago when he acknowledged for the first time the change in himself? He had spent the first half-year on the run, avoiding real and imagined threats, living rough most of the time, using the showers available at truck stops infrequently enough to make him unpleasant to be around.

Not that he wanted to be around anybody. Those brown eyes of hers, their inspection of his soul—a thing she had no right to do—the way he came up wanting, the frankness with which she dismissed him as a worthy opponent at a time last year when she was his helpless prisoner. The Montreal operation failed in every way except one. It reordered his existence, starting with that steady gaze. Now, she sat beside him. Freely. She recognized him and got into the truck anyway.

"I don't know what I should say," he said, glancing at her sideways. He noticed she trembled. He turned his head briefly, saw the struggle she was having, and commiserated. He had wrestled his own demons when her friends rescued her and immobilized him for six hours in a room with blood, corpses, and flies. Not a forgettable experience.

He tried again.

"Look, Christine, we're just going to ride around a little while so I can explain. I'm not going to hurt you. I'm never going to hurt you. Just listen a little and feel free to tell me to fuck off every once in a while. I get it. Right now, you need to breathe. Frank told me about the dog and he's whimpering, so he must be concerned, too. Deep breath. Come on."

There came a shuddering breath ending in, "Fuck off."

He decided it was a good sign. The dog became quiet. Another positive omen. He launched an abbreviated explanation.

"So there was this guy, a tall Asian guy in Montreal. I think you know him. He said he was part of the deep state and gave me money to get away because I killed the guy who wanted to kill you. It made my former—shall we call them associates—want to kill me. That's the summary of a year ago."

Paul took a right onto a forested road along a lake and turned his head to look at her. She breathed normally but stared straight ahead from a perfectly sculpted face, high cheekbones and forehead, graceful curve of the neck under a dark ponytail. He looked away.

"He also gave me a phone number," he said. "It took me six months to call it."

Still nothing from her.

"I spent another month waiting for contact. I used it to think about stuff. Went so far as to become vegetarian."

"Fuck off, Paul."

He had told her she could say it all she wanted but because of his new policy of being truthful with himself, he had to admit silently that if this kept up, he'd soon be more than irritated.

"Communicate," the funny old man with bulging eyes who briefed him had managed to spit out after failed attempts at three or four synonyms. "Tell her the truth. You owe her."

"I still eat fish sometimes," Paul told her, for what reason, God only knew. *I'm communicating.*

No answer. Only internal disgust at how awkward he felt. He swept back the peppery hair on his forehead and took another right turn, checking for tails. Swung the truck around in a dead-end a hundred yards down while kicking himself again. *Way to box yourself in, become a sitting duck.* He needed to spend more time getting familiar with the area. And its accents. The people here sounded more foreign to his Colorado ears than had the upstate New Yorkers.

Back to the business at hand. He decided on direct communication with this angry goddess.

"My real name's Damon, Christine. I know Frank told you that. When it's just us, you can call me Damon, but I don't recommend it. You might use the wrong name at the wrong time. Game name is still Paul like it was in Montreal, but I dropped Smith in favor of Mathews. I also abandoned genocide for vegetarianism, by the way. Like I said; it's been a big year for me." He couldn't help the sound of his voice through gritted teeth.

At the stop sign, she turned to study him. "Fuck off, Paul. Hitler was a vegetarian."

Did he expect open arms? Welcome to the fold? Congratulations on embracing a worldview not predicated on killing large numbers of human beings? He wanted to shout at her. *Give me a break; give me some credit; give me absolution.* He tasted the bile in his throat. Swallowed hard. Refused to make excuses, even to himself.

"I grew up in a family that thought it was his only flaw," he said, voice low.

How to reconcile love for his grandfather with his newfound rejection of everything the man stood for? Not everything. He would keep the man's domestic wisdom, patience, and support for family while rejecting the murderous ideology. Most of all, how could he convince her this new betrayal was noble, not base, a betrayal of an evil idea, not a loving family—though none of them would see it that way—and therefore, worthy of her confidence?

"Your friends—Frank says they go by the name Charlemagne—have assigned me as your assistant, sidekick, factotum, and bodyguard," he continued. "It's part of my penance for what I used to be. I figure they'd be worse enemies than my former friends are, so it's in my best interest to toe the line."

She nodded.

"Which is plenty of support for asking you to trust me."

She scowled.

"And I hereby rescind your license to tell me to fuck off.

She turned to him. "When it's just us, Damon, call me Agaskw. I don't recommend using it until you learn how to pronounce it. You might forget you're the assistant."

He couldn't hide the irritated curl of his lip as he narrowed one eye at her.

Her face lit up with a wicked, belligerent smile.

He jerked the truck back into its lane before it ran out of shoulder heading for a tree. They rode silently the rest of the way to the barn he and Frank had set up for Christine's training in tradecraft.

6

The first thing Christine liked about the small woman who opened the front door to her a few hours later was her attention to Fluffy. "Bring him in with you," said Mary Catherine Rogers. "You cannot leave him in a car in summer, even with the windows down."

The invitation meant Christine would be able to take her time with this interrogation. The second thing she liked about Lew Caslander's girlfriend was the excellent cup of Labrador tea she ladled into a mug from a large pot simmering on the stove.

They sat at the kitchen table. Police had allowed a cleaning service to begin sanitizing the crime scene in the living room, but it was still taped off with only a narrow walkway lined in yellow leading to the staircase. Christine kept Fluffy in her lap as she savored the Indian tea of her childhood and reminded herself to not let nostalgia and sympathy warp her perception as they talked.

Mary Catherine wore her deep brown hair short and neatly styled. A light blue summer blazer over a cream-colored tank and black dress slacks indicated she was going to work that day. Was she that dedicated to the bank where she held a minor managerial position? Christine doubted it.

She began with open-ended questions, to gain trust, and to soften the grief betrayed by red-rimmed eyes.

"How are you doing, Mary Catherine?"

"Not well." Mary Catherine spoke to the tea she held in both hands but did not drink. "I thought I should go to work. It felt better to be doing something, to put on makeup, to try to cover the redness in my eyes." She looked up, making eye contact. "Will I ever be able to go back to the bank?"

"Why not?"

Mary Catherine lifted her chin toward a newspaper on the table, the headline screaming, 'Murder on Indian Island.' "Reporters were here all evening," she said. "The elders kept them away from me. They took turns standing watch over my house—both groups, press and elders. But I could not sleep here. How could I? George James took me to my old auntie on the other side of the island. She let me have her guest room. Then, the elders had to watch two houses to keep people away. "

"That was kind of your aunt to do and also considerate of the tribe."

Mary Catherine nodded sadly, with a wry grimace. "My aunt and I don't get along. I didn't sleep much and couldn't wait to get back here and talk to Joseph."

"Is that your son? Is he here?" Christine glanced through the window of the back door. Only two cars sat in the drive and one of those was hers. Mary Catherine confirmed her son's absence with a shake of her head and the beginning of tears.

"He hasn't been home!" Tears flowed freely down her cheeks. "He came home from work while the police were here. They took him away. To talk, they said. He's still there. Did they talk all night? Can they do that? When they took him they asked me about the swords. Whose were they? How many were missing? When did Joseph buy them?" She looked up at Christine. "Who cares when he bought them? Some were gifts, I said. Just because they're his doesn't mean he used them. He was at work when this happened, but they're holding him still! Why?"

The cop in Christine knew why. The mother in her searched for the softest way to explain they were testing his alibi, trying to break it—for a fast arrest. "Have they talked to you yet?"

"No. The tribe would not let them. We have limited sovereignty here. They protected me, but they had to let the sheriff take Joseph away for questioning."

As the first to interview her, Christine was getting an untainted glimpse into Mary Catherine's world. The bad news was that George's fears seemed justified. The government was doing its best to pin this on her son. The state would hold him while the feds assembled a case.

"Tell me about Joseph," she said.

With another open-ended question, information came in floods of emotion and contradiction. Joseph was a wonderful boy who grew into a fine young man; he was such a boy still, so immature. He loved his mother but never listened to her. Very handsome, anyone would want to marry him. He was never attracted to nice girls worthy of him, only sluts and gold-diggers. Not that he had any gold to dig for but he made very good money. His boss loved him, but he had always been late for school, so had he changed, or was the boss too indulgent? And why wasn't he saving his money the way he should?

Christine wanted to join in, make it a mutual lament with this fellow traveler of motherhood, and tell her about her son, Cody. But Frank had warned her. "Don't tell anyone you have a son, Christine—for his sake. You're in a new place now. Nobody needs to know. Learn the concept 'need to know'. It saves lives."

She had spent the morning with Paul learning the art of secrecy. As a cop, she had always practiced discretion, but she was proud of the uniform, unashamed to openly wear the law enforcement part of her identity. Her new persona would take practice. "Make it your instinct, Christine," Paul had said. "You won't create an intelligence network if your agents are endangered just by being seen with you. Be like Fluffy. Too cute to be dangerous."

He had not yet experienced Fluffy's teeth.

And what did he mean by calling her cute?

7

At Christine's request, George James sat on the backseat of her car in the jail parking lot. Joseph Stinson's alibi had held up for the most part, enough to get him released after pressure from George's pinch-hitting real estate lawyer. She turned to face George and studied his expression, looking for something besides plain annoyance.

"Why can't we talk in my car?" said George.

Because Paul swept this one for bugs and my alarms were still in place when I left Mary Catherine's house.

"I don't want to leave Fluffy any longer than I have to," she said aloud, reading the patient dismissal of her female vacuity in his upward eye roll. *That's a good thing, Frank would say. You want them to think that.*

Paul did say it, using the word cute again. Like thoughtlessness and cuteness go together. And anyway, since when is a forty-five-year-old retired trooper, who has seen it all, referred to as cute?

Fluffy slept in the dog seat that hung from the headrest of the seat next to her. A summer rain—more of a downpour —gave them privacy by streaming down the windows fogged on the inside by their breaths.

"I need to talk to him before anybody else does, George. I'll be careful not to let him incriminate himself. I'm just asking you to bring him here when the police release him. I'll drive him home."

"Are you sure it's a good idea to have him behind you like this, Christine? I mean, what if he did kill Caslander? Move the damn dog, for God's sake."

George narrowed his eyes, changing male modes from underestimating to overprotecting. Not a good thing in a business relationship. No matter how much Frank and Paul counseled about tradecraft, she also needed to establish the private investigator legend. This first client needed more confidence in her.

She put on her most official cop face, scowling with lowered brow, and barked her next words. "I can handle it, George."

"You're not armed...."

"Neither is he. He just got out of jail, remember? Bring him here."

...

"What the hell did you think you were doing letting that kid get behind you?" said Paul from the seat Joseph had just vacated.

Christine sighed, clenched her jaw, and spoke through her teeth. "Trust me to take care of my own security, Paul. Joseph is harmless. And anyway, he wasn't armed."

"You don't have the cop grille between the seats that you're used to. He didn't have to be armed."

"I told you, he's harmless."

"Fluffy didn't think so. He growled at him."

"He growls at everybody. And when were you going to tell me you bugged this car? How much did you hear?"

"I've just now told you, and I heard the whole interview, including the growling. You forgot to ask the kid why he keeps all those blades on the wall."

She pulled the car into the drive-thru at a chain coffee shop on Main Street. "I need coffee," she said.

"So do I. Large. Black. You should have asked about the blades. That's weird."

She ordered and pulled forward to the window. He handed her a ten-dollar bill. She ignored the offer, dug into her jeans pocket, and came up with only a single. She hated that she had to accept the ten still held out to her.

"The sword collection is not weird," she said, taking the change and handing it to him, but he was looking away. Or he ignored the offer. She reached back and poured it into his lap.

"Hey!" He had to loosen his seatbelt to get at the coins under him. "Don't you dare do that with the coffee."

She had to admit the steel in his voice was a little sexy, but she banished the thought. Their history was anything but, and she had learned not to allow ambiguity in her relationships. Cooperative animosity was working for them so far. No need to change it.

She picked up the thread. "It's not weird for a wannabe fighter to collect fancy weapons. He's that type. The wall of swords is normal."

"I never did that."

"You were an actual fighter. You didn't have to pretend." This was an educated guess based on the way Paul moved with understated power. Her career in the force had taught her to recognize a criminal when she saw one, especially a well-trained and conditioned professional.

"Fair," he said, accepting the compliment without surprise.

So I was right.

Paul sipped his coffee and scanned the highway, checking the side mirrors and looking behind as she drove toward the victim's home further up the river in Morgan. "Joseph took an awful long lunch," he said. "Plenty of time. He works ten minutes away. He could have come home, found Caslander there, had it out with him, and apologized for being late when he got back to work."

"He would have been covered in blood. You didn't see the room. No way could he have come out of there and gone straight to work."

"He could have showered and changed. It is his home."

She had to admit to herself that he was right. She made a mental list of things to check on. "Do you think our magic computer can get into the local department's files so I can see the raw reports of their interviews?"

"Yes."

After five minutes of mutually thoughtful silence, he continued, "So now that you acknowledge it was bone-headed to let him get behind you, I expect you to be more careful. That's an order."

"I'm not taking orders from you."

"You are when it comes to security. I have the remit."

"You can't make me. Even if you hit me again."

She watched him wince in her rearview, like the coffee in his cup had developed a sour taste.

8

Paul took a deep breath, told himself her reaction was to be expected, and remembered all that Frank had said. Frank, the funny old wise man, the retired deep-state bureaucrat who knew all the scary things about him and had advice on every subject.

"I've been in the company of you guys all my adult life, my boy," said Frank. "Yours is a past on the wrong side that has to be dealt with. She may or may not come around."

"I'm pushing fifty, Frank, no longer a boy, and I think it's a helluva gamble using me for this. She'll have memories. It can't help but affect us operationally."

And doom any chance I might have with her personally.

"She's met worse than you and managed to get along," said Frank.

Frank wasn't referring to the criminals Christine spent her first career locking away. Paul remembered the snappy dresser who left him in that safehouse with the corpses and flies. The one he met later at his motel room. The one who Frank said had let him live.

Paul shuddered involuntarily because he believed it. He knew it at the time, just looking at the guy, at the stillness of his blue-eyed stare. The man was of his own kind, opposite side, but way better at it. Paul associated the name Charlemagne with that stare but knew it was a collective name, a team name. Frank called him Mack and impressed on Paul the importance of forgetting even that.

He glanced at Christine. She watched his reverie in the rearview, reading the progression of his memories, noting the shudder. He regretted another escaped wince, and cultivated a stone sculpture look, using Mack as his model.

They took the Morgan exit from I-95, drove through a dark green forest for two miles, and came to a stop sign at a T intersection. She hesitated and did not set a signal.

"Turn right," said Paul, congratulating himself on his knowledge of the area. Collecting it had been time well spent.

"You're not trying to make me do a bunch of right turns to check for tails, are you, Paul? There is nobody out here."

"Just turn before you hold up traffic. Caslander's house is on Fourth Street, two blocks from State."

"What are you, a map?"

Fluffy sat up in his car seat when the car stopped. He pointed his nose to the right—like he understood the conversation. Strange dog. Christine made the turn and Paul wondered whose advice she was following, his or Fluffy's?

She pulled into a parking lot around the corner and down two blocks. They walked through a modest New England neighborhood to a run-down, two-story Victorian house with a single-car garage at the back of an overgrown garden. After another low-voiced argument about the dog's participation—which Paul lost—the three of them used the cover provided by the garden to approach the house out of view of the street.

"The dog is too conspicuous," said Paul. Again.

"He makes us look normal. Nobody pays attention to a dog out for a walk doing his business. Act natural."

Fluffy acted natural by making a deposit in the weeds. Paul grimaced, keeping watch while Christine pulled out a plastic bag and did the normal thing. They left the bag and its contents in an overflowing city trash can next to the garage.

He handed her a pair of gloves, donned another pair, and led her to the back door. Choosing a short hook from his tool pouch, he probed the lock, found it deceptively deeper than expected, and changed both strategy and tool. Twice. The dead man knew his locks.

They stepped over pieces of kitchen tile and drywall covering the linoleum floor.

"Joseph couldn't kill the guy and then do this during a long lunch," said Paul as he took in the scope of the damage. "The drive alone...." He turned to Christine. "Could police?"

She shook her head. "They would not mind making a mess, but not like this. Somebody else was looking for something specific. Justin gave me all the initial reports from the local department. There is no hint of any theories about the murder that would require a search of the victim. No suspicion of drugs or other contraband. No trafficking, despite the aviation angle. The cops are concentrating on his love life."

"What aviation angle?"

"Caslander was a pilot. Began life in helicopters. He worked for Air America in Southeast Asia."

"So, once upon a time, he was one of us?"

"Yes, according to Justin. He ran a fixed base operation at the Morgan Municipal Field for the past year."

"And who the hell is Justin?"

"The hacker who works for Charlemagne. Didn't Frank tell you?"

He shook his head. "Remind me to impress upon you once again the concept of need to know."

"You asked me. What was I supposed to say?"

"You shouldn't have brought up his name in the first place. I am deeply concerned you'll start peppering your conversations with my name. Don't."

They toured each room of the house, all of them equally tossed, with walls pierced in likely and unlikely places. Even the floorboards of the unfinished attic had been taken up and the insulation thrown aside.

Christine headed back to the first-floor room the dead man used as an office. Paul felt uncomfortable. They had been in the house too long. They were parked too close. If this was an intelligence-related hit, they needed to move out quick. She had taken Fluffy off his leash, and after nosing through the piles of paper on the floor, the dog was agreeing with him. He whined.

Christine picked up a stapled document of about six pages. "What is this? It looks like it's from a court."

"Yeah, good, let's go."

"Caslander was in a lawsuit."

"Great find. Come on."

She stood, reading.

Paul took her upper arm and pulled her toward the door. She resisted.

Fluffy barked furiously.

They heard a key turn in the front door ahead of them. Christine folded the document in half, slipped it into the waistband of her jeans, and covered it with her t-shirt.

"Take off your gloves," she said. "Quick."

The door opened.

9

Too many threats! Fluffy's fur—all the short strands at the back of his neck—stood vertical. His humans—The Paul had become almost acceptable as one of *his* humans—hid their blue plastic hand decorations in their pockets while a strange, probably dangerous, human came through the front door. Christine swooped Fluffy up into her arms. He knew this as a signal to stop barking but was careful to show his ferocity by displaying his fine teeth. The Paul placed a protective arm around Christine's shoulders. Fluffy tentatively approved, adding the gesture to mounting evidence that classified The Paul as an ally.

Christine turned up her mouth in what Fluffy considered a happy face. It sufficed as a signal in the absence of a tail. Poor, socially ill-equipped species. She said quietly, "Stop growling." Then came the soft sing-song voice, "Everything is fine, Fluffbutt."

This was the comfortable word. The Paul narrowed one eye and wrinkled his nose with a glance at Fluffy, surprised at this mark of respect. Fluffy set his ears forward, alert but relaxed and confident. The man coming through the door opened his eyes wide in surprise. He opened his mouth, too, but Christine was faster.

"Hi, you must be the listing agent? Our agent said she could not reach you and she couldn't stay so you just missed her. We are leaving. I'm not sure the house is worth the asking price, what with the condition it's in. I suppose we can fix it, but not at that price and I don't think I'm up for another project. Work has been so demanding lately. My boss is a real… well, you don't want to hear it. So good luck with the sale. We'll be on our way. Thanks for letting us look. Bye."

They squeezed past him through the old, extra-wide doorway and were down the front stairs before he shouted, "Hey! What the…?"

Fluffy found himself on the sidewalk running beside Christine. He watched her legs stretch beside him. They ran together, and he let his tongue feel the air, licking his nose from time to time to check the scent. The Paul had a strong smell of fight. He smelled dangerous. Christine's scent was full of the strength that comes with emergency. This meant Fluffy was in an emergency. His head bobbed as his hindquarters bunched toward his single front leg at every running step. He moderated the pace to stay even with Christine. She was fast for a human, but he could be faster.

They cut into a backyard, crashed through a hedge. The Paul led them around the back of a restaurant near the dumpsters. The smell was intoxicating. Fluffy would have stopped to enjoy, but the humans were urgent so he conquered the urge.

Paul ran in a sweeping curve back in the direction they had come. Another delectable dumpster in a parking lot—the place where they had stashed the car.

They were still making breathing noises as she started the Jeep. Paul threw Fluffy's car seat in the back and held him on his lap. Fluffy panted, but with exhilaration, not distress. Christine pulled the folded paper out of her waistband and handed it to Paul as she pulled the car into the street.

"Read it. Aloud, please."

"CASLANDER, Lewis, of Morgan, County of Penobscot, State of Maine, Plaintiff…."

Christine blew out an irritated sigh. "Okay, so he was suing somebody. Cut to the chase. Who?

"The city of Morgan, the city council in general, three of the councilors by name, and the mayor by name."

"Why?"

"Interference, harassment, breach of contract." Paul turned over the paper. Fluffy sniffed the new page and found nothing interesting, which was fine by him, because it took so much effort to get them to understand when he knew something was important.

He curled up in Paul's lap and closed his eyes as Paul talked again, turning the papers one by one. Fluffy rested lightly, hearing the sounds made, scanning for important words.

"It says Caslander took over the FBO last year...."

"FBO?"

"Fixed base operation—at the airport. He took over a contract with the city and invested in tools, equipment, staff, and flight instructors. After a few months, the city started dinging him with complaints about the tools, the parking plan, the schedule. The mayor badmouthed the flight school. Flight students left and Caslander lost business. The lawsuit says there is evidence. I imagine it wouldn't be hard to get. If any of this is true, the city council, or at least some of it—especially the mayor—didn't like him."

Christine took the on-ramp to I-95 toward Bangor. The smoother road at high speed lulled Fluffy into semi-consciousness as her words filtered through his large ears.

"That makes three possible angles," she said. "A love-life murder like the police would like it to be—cut and dried. A consequence of his involvement, past or present, in the spook world. And now, a business relationship gone sour."

The car became quiet except for the blinker noise as they passed slower traffic. Fluffy was barely conscious when Christine said, "I want to know why they don't like him. I'm in charge here and have decided you have a need to know. We'll call Justin."

Fluffy sat up. The Justin was an important word.

C hristine hung up the phone, and the printer began. Justin was that fast. She looked up at Paul standing over the machine, one eyebrow raised. He took a sip from an oversized mug of black coffee. An occasional whiff from his direction was not coffee. He needed a shower. Was he living in that barn?

"So this is Justin?" he said, indicating the paper shooting into the tray.

Fluffy raised his head momentarily but tucked his nose under his front paw and went back to sleep on the easy chair.

Christine nodded.

"Where is this guy? Who is this guy?"

"I don't know," she said. "Frank won't tell me. He has a young voice and a way with computers. He works for Charlemagne. That's all I know. Justin is my private NCIC —on steroids."

"NCIC?"

"National Crime Information Center. I'm no longer a cop, and Frank didn't want me to use a friend at my old station for access when he helped me set up my agency. He gave me Justin instead. All I know about him is he's awesome."

"He must be if he works for Charlemagne. What's the area code you call to reach him?"

"An 800 number. And stop prying."

"I can't help loving a mystery. Are you seriously thinking you'll read all this?" Paul indicated the paper in the tray, now almost an inch thick with the printer spitting out more.

Christine pointed to the two-inch binder holding Caslander's life history. "I read that last night. Justin is sending four times as much now, but I should have it done in a few hours."

He took another gulp of coffee as he stared at her, swallowed, and said, "So, you're the brainy type."

"I just read fast."

"Brainy people never admit to it. That's how you know them. Same with spooks."

"Those are not the same thing. Spooks can't admit it. It can kill them."

"True. So can being too brainy. I know people who don't like smart-asses, especially smart-asses with degrees, and they know how to shoot straight. Be careful, Christine."

Is he concerned or just doing his job? Christine studied his expression for a long moment before looking away. *And is my fast reading turning him off, or is it my degree?* The last thought threatened to start a long exploration of her feelings. She didn't have time. She tamped it down, then shut down the laptop and closed it.

"Fluffy and I are going out," she said with a pointed look at Paul.

He ignored it, preferring to watch the spewing paper. The stack now exceeded three inches. "How about I make myself comfortable upstairs and get stuck in to doing some reading there, after you tell me where you're going, who you plan to see, and when you'll be back?"

"Not in my personal space, you're not. None of your business; none of your business; and I'll be back when I'm done." They stood in mutual glare. "How about I mention your excessive curiosity to Charlemagne?" she murmured, still locking eyes with him. "You think they'll be interested?" The shadow behind his slow blink and deep breath gratified her.

"They gave me a task here, Christine. I'm the real deal. Don't worry; they know that."

But it worries you. She remembered the speed with which Mack, Charlemagne's founder, killed a young Penobscot turncoat in Montreal. Eric was dead before he could squeeze the trigger. It happened in an instant, right in front of her, and she never saw the knife he used. Paul had reason to worry. She softened and looked away. Besides, he really needed a wash.

"You can take a shower upstairs, Paul, but read the file here in my office. Just keep the shades down. The coffee maker is over there and you can heat up the pot of tea on the burner. I won't be long."

He picked up the stack on the tray. Plenty to keep him busy and out of trouble, she decided. She picked up her keys and unlocked the back deadbolt.

"That's another thing I need to do," he called after her. "That lock wouldn't stop a bobby pin."

"Thanks for telling me. I'm regretting that I let you stay in the building."

"I could follow you instead."

"Your truck's too distinctive."

"That's why I prefer your black Jeep. Come back soon."

. . .

"I am going to find out why Eric turned, Fluffbutt. We'll start with his mom."

Fluffy had been in the process of preparing the fleece in the bottom of his car seat for a comfortable snooze. The tone of respect halted him. He took his position sitting up, pointing his nose forward, ears large and alert. They were on a mission. A private one. She had ditched The Paul, and he felt a change in her manner. He was to be the only one to know about this. She need not worry. He would never tell.

"Her name is Emily Grantson, Fluff. She doesn't live on the res. She lives in Brewer and is a tiny bit Passamaquoddy, according to my information. Eric's dad is nine sixteenths Penobscot. That's all Justin could find out from documents Eric produced when he enrolled in the tribe. I want to know why Eric turned against his own people. We're at the very beginning of this quest. Let's hope it goes well."

It did not go well.

Christine took Fluffy with her, to soften things, she said. He did not know that word, but assumed it referred to his mighty fierceness. He kept his head up, ears forward as she carried him in her arms. She rang the doorbell and the door opened.

"Mrs. Grantson...."

"You're not bringing that mutt in here," said the woman.

She wore very bright hair, which was what humans called the little bit of fur on their heads. It glinted in the hot summer sun. She was heavier than Christine and looked like she could beat her in a fight. Fluffy grew concerned. He smelled animosity but suddenly found himself locked in the Jeep with the engine running and the air conditioning on. He barked in hysterical protest until Christine came back.

"Stupid damn woman," she said as she reversed the car out of the driveway. "Called me a dirty Indian! Can you believe it, Fluff? Like her first husband, she said. Useless half-breed drunk who left her with a kid and never paid a dime of child support after she married the new man. A white man. Eric was nothing but trouble. Didn't look anything like his half-brothers and sisters."

Christine took a deep breath and used a high squeaky voice, talking too loud—like somebody else—probably like the woman with shiny hair.

"'I told him not to get involved with that reservation,' the bitch said. 'I told him to stick with his job at Border Patrol keeping out the damned immigrants ruining this country, but would he listen? No. And now he's dead and some Indian bitch comes here to tell me you're sorry for my loss? That you saw it happen? And you need information to find out why? It's no loss, lady. It's a blessing. Go back where you came from and leave me alone.'"

She stopped the Jeep at a red light, dropped her forehead onto her knuckles at the top of the wheel, and sobbed. A car behind made noise and she drove on a little calmer, Fluffy was happy to see. Still, he did not like it when her cheeks were wet like that.

"Am I the only one who mourns that kid?" she said aloud just as the box on the console between the seats rang a bell. Fluffy looked down at it. He had never heard it before. The Frank had something to do with it, was involved in putting it there, so he was suspicious He showed it one of his canines. She pulled to the curb and stopped, opened it, and picked up a Justin device.

"Hi, Frank."

The Justin was in league with The Frank! Not good. Fluffy showed all his fearsome teeth to The Justin in the box.

11

"What's wrong, my dear?" Frank had long experience with the signs of emotion in the women of his family. They couldn't hide it from him, even over a car phone signal. Their tears were alien to him, but he suspected it was a healthier approach to trauma than the stoicism men were required to exhibit. His question released Christine's sobbing and he waited for it to subside into sub-blubs before pressing for an answer.

"Tell me."

She did. It was a long tale about toxic parenthood. Prejudice, belittling, and the absence of love. Good foundations for a bad future. He had heard it many times. He cut to the chase and gave the antidote Christine needed.

"Cody is okay, Christine. Your son is doing fine. He loves you. He did not have a mother like this woman. You did well. He is a credit to you."

As a father of seven and grandfather of five and counting, Frank knew all the right words. They were what he would have needed. He just wouldn't have been as watery about it.

Her voice steadied. "It kind of explains it all, doesn't it, Frank? But if he hated his Native ancestors, why did he enroll in the tribe in the first place?"

"He did that as a teenager during the age of rebellion. It's good to have a glimpse into his ment…, his minds…, his psychology, my dear, but it sounds like you think this settles it."

"Doesn't it?"

"No. There is still a bad actor somewhere who will continue targeting others with confused loyalties. That's why you're in Maine. You went there to find that person, as well as to create your own network."

"I haven't even started that. I plugged in all those new electronics only two days ago. The flat is full of unpacked boxes, and this is the first time I've answered the car phone you gave me. And now, I'm supposed to solve a murder?"

Frank was going to have to fly back to Maine. He hoped he could do it alone. There had been a renewal of outside threats headed in his direction. The team might decide they would need to protect him. In person. That would risk the trouble they always attracted. He shook himself and concentrated on the task at hand. Assurance and deflection.

"You will do it all, Christine. It's an incremental process and you've just begun. You can't see it yet, but you're making progress. Everybody here is impressed. Tell me how you're getting along with Paul."

. . .

Christine took a deep breath before answering and hoped it wasn't audible. She felt the pause was too long. He would know she was being careful.

"We're getting along," she said. "He's taught me a lot and he keeps his distance, so that part's okay."

"What part is not?"

Everything. What to admit to the team? She knew Frank was their man. The scary younger dude, Charlie, was probably standing right next to him, listening in all his special brand of silence. She shuddered.

Charlie's father, Mack, was just as terrifying, but only when she thought about it. He looked like a well-dressed older man with a game leg, but he moved so fast, you couldn't see what you were seeing, only the result in the very next second. In Montreal, she had seen her deputy Eric die at her feet, his finger still on the trigger he would never be able to squeeze, the chambered round never entering his target, an advocate for his own people. The young man's blood oozed slowly from deep inside his chest. A glance at Mack revealed a glint of steel, but it was gone before she could process the enormity of this death.

What, or who, prepared Eric to turn traitor, to kill his own? It was in that moment when Christine pledged to find out. Mack and his team, Charlemagne, supported her. The quid quo pro was an essential element of their survival: information. The plan was a symbiosis of shared intelligence between the team and the Wabanaki tribes.

She came to Penobscot County to build a network for her own purposes and for Charlemagne's. They were her allies but not the kind she ever wanted to cross, nor for that matter, come across in a dark alley. And here she was in league with them and with a former enemy, Paul. A personal enemy at that. *Sigh.*

"Christine?" Frank sounded concerned.

"Yeah, I'm here. I can't explain it."

"Do you think he's dirty?"

She could be rid of Paul with one word. But it wouldn't be true.

"No," she said. "Just irritating." A stray internal self-reflection told her she didn't want to be rid of him.

"I suspect he's being overprotective," said Frank. "He'll loosen up when he learns how capable you are. Cut him some slack. Where is he now? I know he's not there with you. I doubt you'd cry in front of him. Am I right?"

How the hell does he read me like that?

"Yes." She hissed air through her teeth before going on. "I left him in my office reading the information Justin sent regarding a possible suspect. I told him not to bring it upstairs to my apartment, but you know he can get in anywhere. Can you get me a better lock? Paul said the victim, Caslander, had a good lock and knew what he was doing. But Paul still got in."

"The man has skills, my dear. I'll try, but I don't think you need to worry."

How would she react if he came in uninvited? Too many scenarios presented themselves, horrifying, unpleasant, uncomfortable, not so uncomfortable, and.... As she ruthlessly shoved the unthought word out of her mind she began to worry.

12

Paul knew she had been crying because of the smeared mascara above one eye. Christine didn't wear much makeup, but she did accentuate her beautiful long lashes—Paul deleted beautiful from that last thought. They were, but thinking it would not be healthy. He concentrated on the mascara and proceeded carefully as she walked past him to the coffee machine.

Fluffy sat down on the floor in front of him and made eye contact. The dog was trying to tell him something. He fancied at first the dog wanted to tell him about the crying, but then realized he was sitting (quite comfortably) in Fluffy's easy chair.

I rank below a ten-pound dog here.

He moved to one of the client chairs in front of Christine's desk and waited. Fluffy took his place and fell asleep immediately. Christine drank half the mug she poured before acknowledging Paul's presence. Red rims under the makeup smear confirmed recent weeping.

"Did you read anything interesting?" she asked.

Whatever had gone before, she was in perfect control now. He could not help but admire her.

"I did. I mostly skimmed it, looking for connections between the council and Caslander. I needed something besides the lawsuit. There's no indication that any of them, the three councilors or the mayor, had anything to do with him before or since he got here a year ago. I checked your

Caslander notebook again also. I'd wanted to find out if one of them had occasion to hold a grudge we don't know about."

Christine sat in her desk chair and pulled out a notebook. "Proceed," she said, uncapping a fountain pen.

He did not appreciate what sounded like an order, but continued, "I looked at addresses and found nothing. Travel history, mostly nothing."

She looked up at him, pen still on the paper, a round spot of ink seeping into the fibers. "Mostly?"

"It's convoluted, but I think the mayor, Bobby Greene, is worth looking at."

"Why?"

Paul cupped his chin and gazed at the ceiling. "Bear with me while I explain. I had a low draft number in 1970, so I joined the Air Force to stay out of the infantry and wound up loading a 105 howitzer in the back of a C-130 gunship stationed in Thailand. My unit worked the Ho Chi Minh trail taking out convoys from North Vietnam. I was eighteen and ignorant, but I remember the setup. Caslander flew over Laos, but he would have been supported in Thailand like we were."

Christine dotted the i in Thailand and looked up again. He went on. "Justin gave us passport information. One of the three councilors has a passport. He was Army and served in Bosnia, but he's too young for Southeast Asia. Greene had a passport at the same time as Caslander."

"Was he drafted? Did he go to Vietnam?"

"No military record. He had a deferment for a sports injury gone wrong."

"But he had a passport? He could have gone anywhere in the world. Why would it mean he knew Caslander?"

Paul shrugged. "It's just a feeling. I get these sometimes and have learned not to ignore them. Like when I met Mack the second time."

Christine stopped writing. "A second time? When?"

"About three months ago. That's how I knew I had turned the corner in my... let's call it my change of mind. Frank called me and said he was picking me up for a conference. He drove me to an airfield and put me on a small jet. The chief pilot was a young redhead, but her co-pilot was a big guy who made damn sure I didn't move. It was night. I don't know where we flew to, but we landed after a couple of hours and the co-pilot delivered me into a back room in a dark hangar."

...

Christine waited, watching for signs of evasion. Change of mind? From racist asshole to what? This guy was a dyed-in-the-wool white supremacist when they met the year before. She had been his prisoner. He hit her, called her names. Now her scary-as-hell allies were vouching for his conversion? As a teenager, the young Eric had rejected his hate-filled upbringing to embrace his Native heritage. What made him turn back?

More important for her, what might make Paul un-convert?

He looked steadily into her eyes like he wanted to say more than the words he was using. She listened, trying to catch the words that weren't there.

"We stood under a bright fluorescent, never even sat down. It was me, Mack in an expensive suit, cane and all, and another guy. He was one of the guys who pulled me off the ground after I killed Smitty, who was going to kill you.

"This guy with Mack was tall, with dark hair, blue eyes, long limbs like a spider. A lot younger than me. Still in his twenties, I'd say. I didn't know why he was there. Mack doesn't need a bodyguard, does he?"

She gave a wry smile and shook her head.

Paul continued picking through words, "Anyway, the twenty-something never said a word while Mack grilled me, searched me through and through, every corner of my consciousness. All I could think was, Why is this spider here?"

Her turn to shrug. "Why?" she said. "And why are you telling me about this?"

He locked their eye contact willing her not to look away. "I'm telling you because for some weird reason, I knew the young guy had the final say in *my* fate. I don't know why I knew but I did. Like I know Caslander and Greene have a connection we haven't found yet."

Did he mention Rimas because of the case or because he suspected her affair? Rimas, an apprenticed mind-wizard in the style of Mack but without the older man's polish, had given her the emotional release she needed during a trying time last year—on a dark day Paul had caused.

13

He had no future. That much was certain. Joseph Stinson, AKA Little Bear, entered adulthood without prospects. The past two days had graduated him from beloved cub of his mother to suspected murderer. He was no longer the hero of his own story; he was the barely sketched bad guy in somebody else's.

The coins in the front pocket of his jeans might be just enough for a coffee. He checked and counted. It was enough. The big-city coffee shop on Central Street in Bangor would be a good place to become anonymous. He couldn't go home.

Bangor Daily News headlines were full of the murder at his mother's—his former—house. He tried and failed to find a table without a copy, settled on a tall stool at the counter in the window, looking out on the street. He pushed the paper over to the space in front of the empty chair beside him.

Somebody took that chair, but he paid no attention and concentrated instead on the liquid in his cup. There was no money for more of it. He had to savor every drop, remember it, mourn it along with all his life up to two days ago. He felt the attention of the man next to him.

"Have you heard of this tragedy?" said the man.

Joseph risked a side glance. Older guy, grey at the temples. Wrinkles. Somehow foreign, maybe Canadian. "Yeah," he replied.

"Disturbing, don't you think?"

Maybe it was the guy's age that made him talk different, too formal. *Formally foreign.* Joseph, smiled inwardly at his mental wordplay. He nodded to be polite, but kept his attention on the dwindling liquid in his cup.

"You seem sad," said the man. "Can I help?"

Surprise made Joseph turn and meet his gaze. He saw concern in the tilt of the head and kindness in the half-smile. Eyes didn't quite match, though.

Is he running equations in his head? Maybe I am. Cut it out.

The guy was well dressed in a lightweight suit, looking like he had money. It made Joe feel all the scruffier with his two-day-old stubble. He knew he must smell.

"I lost my job," he said, not wanting to go into detail. Would-be employers don't want to hear about absenteeism caused by long police interrogations. This guy looked like he might be the employer type. Dim hope made Joseph careful with information.

"I see," said the man. "There may be something I can do for you. What is your name?"

Joseph was sure his name was buried under the headline of the story at the man's elbow, probably with the words person of interest attached. Maybe not. He hadn't read the thing through, being too personally involved to stomach the speculation. Maybe this guy had only glanced at it, too.

"Joseph Stinson."

"How can I reach you?"

Another problem. The police had taken the cellular phone he'd worked overtime to pay for. The last thing he wanted was for this guy to call his mother. He wasn't sure he wanted to go home. Ever.

"The library on Harlow Street," he said. "I'm there most days. Usually in the periodical section."

He pulled that out of his ass. Mom had taken him there once, when he was ten. Most libraries had a periodical section. Probably Bangor's did too. He hoped he sounded thoughtful, trustworthy, employable.

The man stood and offered his hand. Joseph took it, tried to use the right pressure in his grip, conjured a frank, manly smile for the guy, who said, "People call me Rusty. An assistant of mine will be in touch."

Joseph saw him reach a grey car parked outside, then drained his cup and threaded his way through the tables, squeezing past a man close by with his head buried in the newspaper, open to the continuation page of the murder story. The man raised his head and met his eye. He was younger than Rusty, but not by much. It was the challenge that made Joseph notice him. That, and the man's scarred knuckles.

Maybe all those karate lessons Mom had paid for when he was a kid only got him to brown belt, but they did provide a smidgeon of wisdom. This guy was out of his league. Challenge not accepted. Joseph walked out the coffee house door and turned up the street.

...

Paul had heard enough. He finished his coffee before heading to the periodical section at the library.

14

C hristine wore her new uniform on this, her first official day on the job. Business-woman civvies, neutral shades of black with a grey-scale print blouse and a splash of red in a light scarf around her neck.

Heaven only knew what the hell Paul was doing. He checked into the office, took the last cup of coffee from the pot, drank two gulps between her lectures, and left after demanding to know her plans without telling her anything about his.

Her creased black slacks already showed a few white Fluffy-hairs. She considered using the lint roller, but discarded the idea as being premature. There would only be more by the time she got out of the car. She put the roller in the outside pocket of her shoulder bag with a notebook and pens. The main part of the stealth bag was reserved for Fluffy.

As she pulled into the Morgan City Hall parking lot, Fluffy looked up from his box in the passenger seat, yawned, curled, and went back to sleep. A morning drizzle kept the outside temperature cool for a summer day. Christine elected to let him sleep, cracked the windows, and left her bag behind. She checked for dog hair, put on the light green designer blazer she bought the day before in a discount store, and walked through a glass door marked 'City Clerk.'

"No," said the clerk. "They aren't here. Nobody, besides me and the accountant has office hours. Everybody else in leadership is part time. We're not a big city. You might try Bridgewater Kia on Main Street. Ask for Don Kerrick. He's president of the Council. He works in the parts department."

Don wore a company ball cap and a full beard. "I'm working," he said.

It was plain he was doing nothing of the kind, unless working involved coffee, an apple fritter, and feet on the desk. Christine prepared for a fencing match.

"I left several messages at City Hall. Perhaps you didn't get them?"

"I got 'em." He took another bite of the fritter.

"I'd like to set up an appointment...."

"My schedule's full."

"I appreciate that you are a busy man, Mr. Kerrick. Perhaps a question or two now?"

"I don't have time and I don't know anything." He took a long pull on his coffee mug, glanced at her, glared.

"You are named in a lawsuit brought by a murdered man," she said, her voice modulated but firm enough to carry a sharp edge. "Have the police spoken with you yet?" She was gratified by his reaction.

He put down the mug, took his feet off the desk, stood and approached. "What are you suggesting?"

He meant to intimidate and he had the height and weight to prevail, but she doubted he had any skill. Most of his weight was accumulated in the belly. She took the stance Paul showed her during their workout the day before. Kerrick would have difficulty if he tried anything.

"I'm not suggesting anything, Mr. Kerrick. I'm asking what you knew about Lewis Caslander before he took over the FBO. Did he have a history of bad business dealings? I presume you were surprised at the lawsuit after less than a year."

Maybe the stance, or perhaps it was the deliberate whiff of suggestion that the city was not at fault that produced an answer.

He shook his head. "He looked okay on paper and we were desperate. Well, the mayor was. He's got this airplane out there and when the old FBO folded, services were, like, really bad. It costs a mint just to keep up with the fuel regulations."

Christine tried not to sigh with relief, masked a smug look of victory before he could notice. "When did it start going sour? Caslander alleged harassment. That couldn't come out of nowhere with the contract less than a year old."

Kerrick shrugged as though genuinely mystified and threw his head back to find an answer on the ceiling. He lowered his chin to look at her with a wrinkled brow and one eye squinted, both puzzled and enlightened at the same time.

"Within a month! We had complaints about his management right away."

"And before you entered the contract, you had no idea he would be a problem?"

"None." He shook his head slowly. "He had great references. His company checked out. He was moving here from North Carolina and Spectre Aviation had a great reputation down there."

"That's right. There *was* a d/b/a on the lawsuit, I recall. So nobody knew about Caslander himself, I gather."

This was the real question, the one she had come to ask. She made sure he couldn't hear a question mark at the end of it.

"No."

She waited and another realization showed as his brow rose, opening his eyes both literally and figuratively.

"Wait. That's not true. Bobby knew him, I'm pretty sure. We had a get-together in the hangar when he got here and they talked like they knew each other."

"Bobby?"

"The mayor. Bobby Greene."

"So, they were old friends?"

He paused, head tilted, and spoke slowly. "I wouldn't go that far."

"More recent then. I shouldn't have assumed they were old friends."

He shook his head. "No. I don't mean that. It did feel like they went way back but they weren't, like, friends. They were real careful, didn't say much." Kerrick held his head at an angle, eyes squinting. "We were all talking, having a beer, maybe five of us, thinking we were there to have a good time. But it felt to me like we were intruding on their not-so-good time, if you know what I mean?" He looked for her nod of understanding before continuing. "The others musta felt it, too, cuz I've never known anybody to leave a party without finishing their beer."

"They didn't finish?"

"Everybody set down their bottles and left when the party got kinda damp and limp. My wife cleaned up. She said every can had to be poured out. Like the party kinda just poured out.

15

P aul had news to give and a job to do. He suppressed the urge to start talking and instead began their workout, forcing the agenda. She tried to talk. He ramped up the reps until she had no extra breath. She was inexcusably late to the barn and became visibly angry when he refused to listen. It gratified him that she let him have it during their sparring session.

Still smarting from where her fist glanced off his jaw, he veered sideways to evade an attempted knee to the groin, put one leg behind her, and brought her down. She kept fighting, kicking at his lower legs, twisting in an effort to stand, and tripped him to the mat where it became a wrestling match. She was making progress. He used both weight and position to pin her shoulders. They paused in mutual heavy breathing—of the less desirable kind.

Paul waited for her to let go the anger.

"Okay. Session over. You win," he said when she stopped straining.

"How can I be the winner when I can't move?"

"I'll let you move when you're calm enough to accept the win."

"Again, how is this a win?"

"Because you get to go first. I can see you want to talk. I will listen. Let's drink some water and you can give me your news. Deal?"

Paul kept a defensible position as he let her up and handed her a towel. She grinned at him as she took it.

"I got you good," she said, pointing to his lower cheek. The grin widened.

"Just a glancing blow. Don't get cocky."

"It's turning color. That it's not broken is your fault. You're the teacher."

Warring emotions tightened his sore jaw until Paul understood what Mack had done to him by putting this woman in his path toward reclamation. Infuriating and endearing, like many woman he had met, but more complex, more human, or maybe that was in him. That's it, he decided. She makes *me* human. The newly formed humanity in him both urged him and restrained him from shaking her.

He sat on the bench and looked up at her. "Proceed. What's your news?"

"You were right. Caslandar and Greene met before."

He nodded, accepting the victory of an *I told you so*. "What else?"

"That's all. Confirmation comes from the president of the council, who could be lying, could be covering his own tracks, except for the way he said it, like it was a sudden revelation. He told me about a party they threw to greet Caslander when he first arrived. Greene didn't shake his hand." She took a long pull from her water bottle and used her towel to wipe her face before continuing.

"I went into some detail with him about their body language. He used the word careful. Caslander smiled, more like a smirk, Kerrick said, and Greene kept scanning the room. Like he wanted to run. Well, Kerrick didn't say that part, but I did some round-the-room eye sweeps for him and he picked the one I titled, *Who's Watching Me?*"

She took a longer pull on her water bottle.

"That's not evidence," said Paul.

"Not of guilt," she said nodding. "Or even involvement. So far, it's only an indication you might be worth listening to. So, tell me your news."

Paul draped his towel across the back of his neck to give himself time to consider how much to tell her. She would need it all, he realized, but how to phrase things without reminding her about their first encounter. He didn't want her to remember that. *He* didn't want to remember it.

"Remember Montreal?" He kicked himself internally, but there was no hope for it. After her cautious nod, he continued, "I'm not sure how much you knew about what happened there."

"I know you were evil. Maybe you still are. I don't know why Mack didn't kill you."

"Neither do I. But back then, as you will recall, I worked for a nasty organization.

"And now you work for a saintly one?"

He paused, gritting his teeth at the sarcasm. "Nobody in this business is clean, Christine. You cops think your souls are lily white, but you share all the traits of the nasties you go up against. The more power you exercise, the more it damages you. Maintaining a moral code starts with one or two clear lines but ends in a jumble of dots. I'm a dot. You're a dot. The kid, Joseph Stinson, is a dot. And he met a jagged piece of rock today."

He saw her drop the sneer when he said that name. For her, it's all about the kid, he decided. "I met a guy in Montreal," he said, "and today he met Joseph."

"You're saying Joseph killed Caslander in some kind of intelligence hit?"

"I'm not saying that at all. Take a minute to listen, will you? Joseph is only now being recruited. If he did the murder, it wasn't about intel. If it was intel-related, then Joseph didn't do it."

Paul watched her pace as she marched a circuit around the sparring mat, throwing her head back during a momentary pause. Maybe the ancient rafters of the barn inspired thought. He suspected not but looked up involuntarily to see what she saw. He saw bat guano on the cross bar support.

She dropped her chin and looked at him. "It's neither."

"So you don't want to know about the recruitment?"

"I do. But not for this case and not now. It's time to learn all we can about Mayor Greene." She wrinkled her nose. "We'd better clean up if we're riding together. Or you can stay in the office and contact Justin."

Fluffy picked up his head and curled the lip over his left canine.

"He'll talk to me?" Paul did not try to hide his well-founded skepticism. It had been only six months. He would not trust such a fundamental change in a man in so short a time. "You know, your backers might take a chance with your life, but they're not going to let me have access to anything that touches them. They're scary dudes. I'd rather not get crosswise."

"I cleared you with Justin. He won't let you have anything that doesn't have a bearing on this case."

"You have that kind of power? Do you know anything about him? Like where he is?" Paul hoped fervently Justin was not local.

She shook her head. "He's male and not old and he can find anything in a computer, nothing else."

He looked at her, mouth open. She was female and not old and backed by power and used to power. Soft and small and dangerous as fuck. He closed his mouth and nodded. "I'll be at the office in fifteen."

16

The scent was familiar. So was the mess. Fluffy did not, as a rule, mind messes. A tasty morsel could lurk under every pile of paper spilled from a desk or filing cabinet. Something left behind, maybe old and a little bit rotten and delicious, or old and a lot rotten and a delight to roll in. He liked to decorate himself with interesting smells.

Fluffy did not like the strength of that other scent, the one he recognized from the old house that time a stranger came through the door and they ran to the car. He enjoyed the running, but not the fear.

He whined and cocked his head, concentrating on sounds. Christine stopped looking under the counter and became still, not making a sound as she turned her head in the direction of Fluffy's ears.

He heard a breath being breathed and let loose his opinion of stealthy breathers.

The man stepped out from behind a door. Fluffy could see tall tables behind him, tall enough to be hiding other men. Nothing about this place was good. He took his fiercest stance and prepared to let the man have more of his opinion. He knew he could be very intimidating and could feel the danger in Christine's tension behind him. He again raised his nose and opened his mouth, throat ready, chest heaving.

"Hshhh." It was tense but not loud and Fluffy recognized it. He and Christine had been practicing this sound. He froze as a memory of supreme deliciousness from a can of smelly sardines intruded. Such boons came only with silence. He was duly silent. But vigilant. Ever vigilant, fur bristling, canines gleaming in full view under his raised lips. There would be a reward and he still might get to bite this man.

"Who the hell are you?" said the man.

"Are you Mr. Caslander?" said Christine.

She sounded relaxed, but from the corner of his eye, Fluffy could see the pointy thing she had used to open the door. She held it in her fist with the point to the outside, facing behind. Humans were deficient in natural weapons, but his Christine had chosen an iron tooth that might serve. Fluffy maintained his stance.

"What the hell are you doing in here?" The man took a step forward.

Fluffy gave a low warning growl and he stopped.

"I'm here to sign up for flying lessons. We spoke last week, Mr. Caslander. I'm Christine Barton." She glanced at the open boxes, spilled drawers and paper strewn about the room. "Is something wrong? Has there been a break-in?"

Humans had mobile faces, Fluffy knew, and he watched this one's for signs of aggression. The eyes squinted like in sunlight, but they were indoors. The nose wrinkled on one side with the cheek up and lip curled at the corner. Fluffy read this correctly as a mammal trying to show his canines. He growled in response.

So did the man. "Get out."

"Mr. Caslander, I...," Christine's voice came out soft and extra female—for her.

"Caslander's dead. Get out."

The man lifted one arm, finger pointing to the door, then stepped forward again and shoved Christine.

Fluffy launched, missed, fell, was kicked, yelped, and satisfyingly bit—after Christine threw the man to the floor.

It was the man's turn to yelp.

Christine sat on his back, his arm twisted behind.

"If you're not Caslander, who are you?"

"I'm important in this town, you filthy bitch, and I'll have you arrested for assault and that mutt of yours put down as a danger to the public."

"You assaulted me, Mister Important, and abused my dog. And I'm willing to bet you tossed this place as well. What are you looking for?"

"None of your damn business, Missy. Caslander's dead and you'll have to go somewhere else for your lessons. Let me up and you get the hell out. Assault and trespass. Leave before I call the cops."

Fluffy heard capitulation in the man's voice. He and Christine had won this battle and the man knew it. He remained on guard as she let go. The man was still scowling, but without an active snarl. Christine acted very female, with sweetness in her voice, but Fluffy would not blame the man for distrusting a female who could bring down a much larger human.

Of course, she did it with Fluffy's help. They were a pack.

17

"So who was it?" Paul asked her as she checked the printer for news from Justin. He stood by the counter and pressed the button to start the coffee machine.

Ignoring his question seemed good policy to Christine until her eye caught a line at the bottom of the latest page she lifted from the printer. She turned to him and countered with a question of her own.

"Have you seen this?" She waved the paper at him. He took it from her and spent too long getting to that bottom line, so she enlightened him. "Greene was married to a secretary at Air America. He was there. In Thailand."

"I asked you who was the guy at the airport? Did you ID him?"

"I'm pretty sure it was Greene. He was searching the place and Fluffy recognized the scent as we walked in."

"How do you know that?"

"He opened his mouth with his nose up and curled his upper lip. It's what he does when he wants to find a specific smell. For general smells, he puts his nose down. In this case, he identified a threat."

"Fluffy identifies everything as a threat. Well, except for food and you."

Christine glanced meaningfully toward the coffee. "The place was a mess—very much like Caslander's house was. The guy was rummaging in the flight planning room when I walked in. I pretended I was there for lessons. He was belligerent."

The last burble announced a fresh pot. Paul turned and poured a cup. "How belligerent?"

"Fluffy thought he was attacking when he put his arm up to point the way out."

"Fluffy thinks handing you a cup of coffee in the morning is an attack."

His arm held the pot suspended over a cup. He was taking way too long. Christine involuntarily checked his right hand to see if yesterday's tooth mark showed signs of healing. It was less red. She had to admit the Fluffbutt could be overzealous. She picked up the cup Paul put down next to the printer. The man learned fast.

"I used it," she said.

"It?"

"The noise from the dog and the edgy behavior of the man. I took him down right away." She paused, reluctant to say it but knowing she must. She had plenty of experience with take-downs as a cop, but Paul's method proved superior. The subject had been huge.

Paul almost spoiled the moment by looking smug, with only the left corner of his mouth struggling to smile. But—*credit where credit is due.*

"Thank you," she said. "Your method is effective."

Both corners came up to a smile, not a grin, but sufficiently boyish to make her regret giving the compliment. "Why do you think it was Greene?" he asked again, as he poured one for himself.

"Because he threatened me with the law for the assault and backed down immediately when I countered it with a lie. We both knew he hadn't attacked me. He didn't want complications. He'd been caught tossing the place and he knew it."

"Strange behavior for the upstanding chief citizen of Morgan, Maine, wouldn't you say?"

"Did Justin send you a lot of info?"

"A lot of nothing," Paul said after a sip that made him grimace. "The guy is squeaky clean."

"Any pictures?"

He picked up a slim notebook from a corner of her desk and handed it to her. "First page."

She flipped it open. "That's him." She studied the picture on the first page while taking a sip from her mug. It was cold. She hated cold coffee. Her impulse was to empty it in the downstairs sink and refill the mug, but a growing random thought arrested it. She looked up at Paul. He had tied his greying hair back into a neat ponytail. He taught her to take down a man almost twice her size. He could be useful. He was an operative. A dangerous one. Boy, he could finesse a lie. But did he even own a sport coat?

"I'd like you to inquire about the FBO," she said. "The city will need to lease the airport again now that Caslander's dead. Can you create a credible legend?"

He winced. "You mean wear a suit and act like I've got money? Yeah. Believe it or not, I clean up okay. I'll rent a car, and book a hotel. I'll need shoes. That's what Frank calls them. You know, credit card, license and all that stuff in the legend name."

Christine nodded. "I'll call Frank."

Fluffy picked up his head from his curled position in her desk chair and growled.

"What, exactly, are you looking for?"

"The real Bobby Greene. We know he hasn't done anything to make himself unpopular, but what has he done that makes people vote him into office—how many times now?" She looked up with eyebrows raised.

"Four. There are no term limits in Morgan."

"Why do they like him? The man I met was not likable."

Paul shrugged. "Maybe they're afraid of him."

"Find out. And pick up a new coffee maker on the way back. This one's not working."

He nodded. "Sure thing, boss lady."

She suppressed a smile. His tone was too ironic to be considered a touchdown, but it was at least a first down.

18

P aul walked into city hall feeling less than genuine. The sensation surprised him. He had been a subversive for so long, you would think he'd wear this chameleon shit like an old favorite t-shirt. Plenty of past situations had called for an act, a move, a look, to blend or intimidate or escape. But he only ever wore a suit to friends' funerals. He'd even given up church on Sundays, though that was where he once pledged his soul to Christian Identity.

His excuse for not attending worship was his secret work. The real reason was he could take only so much righteousness—in himself and in others. Well before he changed sides and joined the fight against his former friends, he could not pretend to be respectable. Now, he was all he once had been with the addition of being a turncoat. It doesn't get more disreputable than that.

The woman at the counter wore a flowered blouse and a name tag labelled Daisy. She smiled at him, took his legend name, and directed him to the mayor's office.

"The mayor?" he asked with a return smile. "Is he in charge of the airport? I really need to talk to the people—it's probably a committee—who handle the FBO contract."

"The mayor has taken charge temporarily." Daisy had been cute in her day, which was about twenty years ago. Dimples accentuated that fetching smile. It seemed a little more than friendly.

"But does he have sole authority to agree to the contract?" Paul asked, careful to maintain distance, controlling any return smiles, not using her name.

"No," she said, biting her lower lip and no longer hiding a desire to flirt. "We had a bad experience with the last contract; the city wound up in a lawsuit. The mayor is determined to make sure that doesn't happen again. To talk to the committee, you have to go through him."

This was not entirely welcome information. Paul wanted to start with the committee to get a feel for their opinions of this guy—a long-shot murder suspect. Meeting him too early might not be helpful. Still, take advantage of what's on offer, he decided. He'd start with what was in front of him.

"Sooo," he said, donning a promising smile. "Anything I should know about His Honor to help me get that contract?"

She took it in with delight and returned it full of twinkle and dimples. He was disgusted with himself, then surprised. *When did I develop a conscience?*

She dropped her voice in a conspiratorial tone. "Mayor Greene is a very great man. A hero. He never lets on, but everybody knows he was important in the war."

"Which war?"

"Vietnam. He flew airplanes and did secret stuff. That's why he cares about the airport. He still flies his own airplane."

"Big airplane? Little one?"

"Oh little. One of those propeller kinds. He's very humble. He flies just for fun and takes people up to see their houses from the air."

"Have you been up?"

"Oh, yes! Everybody in the office has been. The airplane only has two seats, so when you go, you get to sit right up front. He takes time for everybody. It's so impressive to watch him. When it was my turn, we landed at Bangor Airport and he knew just how to talk to the tower and everything. He took me to lunch after."

It was the wistful tone of the last sentence that made Paul ask, against his better judgment, "Is he married?"

Her face fell. "Yes."

Paul waited, but there was no more information about the mayor's love life, other than the disappointment on her face that told him she wasn't part of it. When she glanced at his ringless left hand he attempted a seductive smile, hoping it wasn't ghastly, and was rewarded by the blush across her freckled nose. He made a mental note to get a ring for his legend. In this case, the lack of one was proving useful, but you never knew when it might come in handy.

He took Daisy to lunch.

...

"What's that on your ear?" Christine sat behind her desk and stared at his left ear. Paul reached for it, couldn't feel anything, tried to remember what might be there. When he took his hand away, the magenta smear on his fingers reminded him.

"Nothing," he said, wiping his fingers on his pant leg. He took one of the two client chairs in front of the desk. Fluffy curled up in an afternoon sunbeam beside the desk.

Christine's tongue bulged her cheek, the eyebrow above it rising in a question mark. She wasn't buying it. What was he supposed to do? Practice celibacy while he waited for her?

Paul watched that thought flit through his mind. *Wait for her? Does that mean I want her?* He knew he was fascinated by her, by the depth in her gaze, the beauty of her face, with its high cheekbones, dark eyes, full lips.... He cut that line of thought ruthlessly and changed the subject.

"Greene is universally respected in Morgan," he said. Daisy had gushed admiration for the man. During lunch at a busy local diner, she also introduced him to other denizens of the town, some of them prominent, all of them complimentary about their mayor. "They think he's flawless and a war hero."

"Justin can't find any record," she said.

"There are units that mask a veteran's service. Special ops units."

"He had a high draft number, and no record of military service at all."

"So maybe he was a deep spook for some other agency —like Frank."

Christine shook her head as she leafed through a half-inch stack of paper held together by a bulldog clip. She opened to a page and handed it across the desk. "He accompanied his first wife to Thailand," she said. "She was the one who worked as a secretary for Air America. Remember?"

Paul glanced over the text. "Their employees were supported by Udorn Air Base, near Laos."

"Was that where you were stationed?"

"No. We were at Ubn, further south." He looked up. "Justin is sure?" He ran over the extensive reading he had done the day before into the life of Lew Caslander. "The murdered guy had a helicopter rating—Hueys. That fits with his Air America record. He also would have been at Udorn. So, if it's Greene who sliced him up, why? What could have happened in Thailand to give him reason decades later?"

"Maybe an affair?"

"You mean he harbored a grudge all this time because Caslander bonked the wife he divorced a few years later? I don't think so."

"What then?"

Paul squinted to narrow his field of vision, to transfer that level of scrutiny to all he had learned from Justin's research. "That means digging up old bones like an archeologist," he said. "We already have everything in the records there is on him. Anything else will be speculation. I don't see how...."

"That's it, Paul." Christine stood and took her car keys from the top drawer. "Thank you. You're right. We have to dig."

"How? Where?" He followed her and Fluffy through the door and to her car.

"To the same hole Greene has been digging in. We need to find the artifact he's been looking for."

"That won't necessarily mean he's the killer. And if I read you right, you're proposing to do breaking and entering again. Dodgy occupation for a former cop."

"True." She turned up her chin with a mischievous smile. "But we won't know either way until we find it. Pick me up here at midnight. We'll take your truck."

"It might be better to rent a car," he said, trying not to think about the trouble she could get into during the next nine hours. He determined to tail her and wouldn't even have time to get out of this god-awful suit and tie. She started her car. As he turned to hurry to his truck, she opened her window and called out to him.

"You know, there's lipstick on your other earlobe, too."

19

C hristine left Fluffy vigilant in his raised car seat box, locking the Jeep still running with the air conditioning on. She did not plan to be long. Mary Catherine's car was parked next to her little cape house by the river. Christine composed a line of questions as she rang the bell.

Mary Catherine did not want to talk about Lew Caslander. Her lip quivered, voice so low Christine had to lean over the kitchen table to hear her.

"Joseph has taken a new job!"

Christine tilted her head. "Isn't that a good thing?"

"No!" Mary Catherine whispered, face full of woe. "They're sending him away for training." Tears began. "He'll meet some girl. I just know he will." A full-on sob.

Christine had trouble understanding, not just the sob soaked words, but the sentiment they conveyed. She would be delighted if her son, Cody, met a girl. He might back off the dangerous profession he had chosen. And there was always the allure of grandchildren, though she considered herself too young for that just yet.

"Is he attracted to unsuitable girls?" she asked, intending to ask for a definition of unsuitable in her next question.

"They've all been gold-diggers, after money, not at all capable of taking care of him."

"All? He's twenty. How many have there been?" Christine pictured a modern day Casanova, crowds of ruined young women populating Penobscot County, Maine.

"Three," said Mary Catherine. "They've all been bad for him, but the first one was the worst. They were too serious. I had to step in. She made him wear nice clothes, and I'm sure she pressured him into *it*.

"*It?*"

"You know... *S E X!*" My boy was brought up in purity before God. That conniving woman was after his money, I told him. He finally came home where he belongs, but then it happened again...."

Mary Catherine gave a detailed account of how she rescued Joseph from each evil influence. It was exhausting, she said.

So was listening to this. Christine found herself contemplating the anomaly of a young man whose girlfriend had to pressure him into something called *it*. "He has money?" she asked, glancing around the simply furnished small house.

"He has everything I have. He's a good boy and he works hard. He knows how to save. I don't want strange women coming along and taking it all from him. I've told him that. He needs to stay here."

Christine put her mug of tea on the table. "With you." Deadpan, not needing to ask because she was beginning to see.

Mary Catherine dipped her chin in a yes of course gesture.

"What did Lew think about Joseph?"

"What do you mean?"

Christine's thinking was evolving now that the dead man had been involved with a woman intent on purity. The sweet little woman on the other side of the table morphed into another toxic mother. Not vicious and insulting like

72

Eric's, but still damaging. This one smothered, dominated, clung.

"Did Lew and Joseph get along?"

The pause felt ominous. Mary Catherine bit her lower lip, took in a noisy deep breath through her nose. "Lew said he liked Joseph, but it wasn't the way he should. He had strange notions about what Joseph needed."

"Like?" Christine leaned forward over the table, trying to catch every softly voiced word, decided the softness itself was a mask, a way to cover an underlying maladjustment. It was affected. She no longer trusted the woman, but filtered her next words through this new understanding.

"Like having his own place! Joseph wanted an apartment. Lew actually encouraged him, said he should strike out on his own. 'Be a man,' he said. Can you believe it? Telling my son to abandon me! I couldn't have that."

Christine remembered the bloody room, the blank space on the wall where the sword had hung.

"So what did you do?"

20

"So what did she do?" Paul said, turning from the computer keyboard when Christine told him about the interview with Mary Catherine. She unloaded a sack of coffee, filters, and a box of assorted European cookies on the counter next to the coffee maker.

"What are you doing on the computer?" she said instead of answering.

"Trying to connect with Justin."

"You can't. You're not authorized yet." She picked up the empty coffee pot and stepped toward the little sink next to the counter.

"You said Mary Catherine did something that changed everything. What did she do?" Paul did not try to hide his exasperation. He'd had enough of being odd man out. Time for straight answers.

I get why I'm not trusted, but how the hell am I supposed to function in a void?

"She dumped Caslander," said Christine. "He interfered with her plans for her son. It means the kid is one notch lower on the suspect list. He had no reason."

"Do you think she killed Caslander, then?"

Christine poured water into the coffee maker before answering. Paul liked her ability to focus on the task before her. If he made the coffee, he would keep talking and slosh water all over the small countertop.

"There is no way she could lift that sword, let alone swing it at him," she said as she pressed the switch to start the brew. "She has motive, but no physical capacity. Her power is quiet and subversive and directed at just one man, her son. She calls it love. Joseph has the physical strength, but no motive. Caslander was helping him escape."

"Escape his mother?" Paul remembered his mother, a tired rag of a woman, helpmeet to his demanding father, bearer of the burdens of off-grid living, who always tucked him in with calloused hands but a soft touch, until she slipped away on a Sunday morning after worship. She was last seen heading down a steep mountain path, nothing in her hands, no pack, no provisions. He tried to follow, but his father said no, and he was left to wonder and watch for telltale buzzards.

He sighed as Christine allowed him to look into her deep brown eyes again, the revolutionary depths he had first encountered a year ago in Montreal. He wondered briefly if she had any children.

"Being a mother is a whole lot of things, Paul. Nobody has a patent that guarantees what anybody would call success, and everybody has a different opinion on the definition. My personal dictionary lists health and happiness of the child in the second and third definitions, both of them subject to the first: the ability to write his own story, using his own words."

So, that meant she did have at least one, and it was a boy. That much came clear to Paul. Childless himself, he avoided theories of child-rearing. He had only memories of how people treated him in the isolated mountain compound where his father administered justice with his fists and his grandfather tempered the severity and bandaged the damaged. The combination formed him; the contrast made him think—an activity his father very much discouraged. Gramps brought a just humanity to his grandson's character, an outlook he must have remembered from an earlier period that valued difference and spirit— but only in white people.

The last noisy sputter of the machine hid the sound of his second sigh, but she acknowledged it with a slight nod. *Tamp it down. She sees too clearly.*

"Mary Catherine considers herself the sole author of her son's adulthood," she said, taking two semi-clean mugs from the shelf. "He is allowed only minor edits that do not interfere with his devotion to her."

Paul wanted to ask her a dozen personal questions. She was a puzzle without solution in his experience. *Same as me, but different.* A thing he had no reference to when growing up, because of what his family called purity of ideology. He was only beginning to appreciate the messiness of humanity.

He accepted the proffered mug filled with hot nectar of the gods, and—after a satisfying sip that burnt his tongue—stuck to business. "So you disagree with my recruiting him? He's the first agent in your network. I thought you would be pleased. Your first agent is a double. Quite a coup."

"Oh, I agree, though I don't think that guy you met in Montreal is one of our targets."

"I met Rusty when he hired my people to take out that Indi... the Native troublemaker... uh, rights advocate you were protecting." Paul searched for more careful words with one side of his lips curled into an apologetic half-smile. "I'm learning new vocabulary here."

He took a deep breath and a deeper pull on his coffee before continuing. "I'd say if Rusty ordered that hit, he's got to be a target of your new network. You're creating an archive of threats against Native Americans. He tried to kill a Native activist. *Air-go* he's worthy of a file folder, at least. Wouldn't you say?"

Christine brought the mug to her lips but put it down again, narrowing one eye in doubt. "And he's trying to recruit Joseph?"

Paul nodded.

"Do you think he turned Eric?"

"Who the hell is Eric?"

Her face clouded, expression closed as she gulped what must by now be cold coffee. "A dead boy," she muttered.

Paul knew there had been more action last year in Montreal than he knew about. During his desperate scrabble in the dirt, before he prevailed over the nut job trying to kill Christine, he heard commotion and sirens close by where the target activist was due to speak. Was the siren he heard for Christine's son? The Montreal operation changed everything for him, made his friends into enemies, set in motion a revolution in his mind.

No. The revolution came before then, when he noticed her soul, a thing he had been taught was impossible in a non-white without European descent. Mental upheaval rose again now, like a mushroom in the littered forest floor of his emotional life.

She has a life. A past. Her own worries. Like me.

He dampened the threatening cascade of further mental change for the momentary sake of the present and told Christine, "Rusty's paying for the basic education of your new double agent. Never look a gift horse, you know. Also, I had Frank's approval before I approached Joseph."

"If I am in charge of this venture, the approval is only mine to give. Or not give."

Paul had no answer. The bloody woman was right. He bit his upper lip, but she said nothing, only stood, her head tilted slightly to one side, demanding his response with a hooded stare.

He reflected the challenge back to her. "And in your absence?"

77

21

Fluffy growled when he heard that voice. It came from the little compartment under the radio where Christine stowed a small object after pressing two buttons. Fluffy could count to three. Well, not everything. But he knew when an amount was more than or less than his feet.

"Paul was in the moment, on the spot, Christine," said The Frank's voice. "You'll have to forgive him." There was a silence. Then, the hated sound came again. "And forgive me."

"We agreed this was my operation, Frank. He didn't even try to contact me."

"Now that you each have one of the new cellular phones, that should not happen again. I assume you made that clear to him. How did he take it?"

"With a stone face, like any man not used to taking orders from a woman," she said under her breath.

"What was that?"

"Nothing. Is this thing secure, Frank? And what about the car phone?"

"More secure than wires at the moment, only because of the volume of data, but anything can be hacked, so keep watch on your topics."

They made a lot of noise, these humans. Why Christine kept talking to things without smells mystified Fluffy. Was The Frank inside that little metal thing with buttons? He remembered that night with the round-shaped old human. His beloved had deserted him, left him confused and alone in that strange house, at night, with other humans he didn't know. He voiced his complaints. Humans made noise all the time, why shouldn't he?

The Frank shouted words at him. Some of these sounds he knew but ignored, words like "No!" and "Stop it!" Then, the old man chased him to a corner and swooped him up in his arms. Fluffy bit his hand.

"Damn dog!"

But The Frank did not let go. He climbed a lot of stairs, making pounding noises on the bare wood, opened a door, and shoved Fluffy inside a dark place with dust and interesting rodent smells.

Fluffy shouted displeasure until his throat hurt, then sat before the closed door, bereft. Eternity passed before it opened and Christine was there. He leapt into her arms, his whole body participating in his joy, from his hoarse voice to the tail that drove the rest of him into motion.

The equations in Fluffy's life were simple. The Frank equaled hardship and privation. Christine embodied comfort and joy and dinner. She had to be protected. He increased his vigilance, scanning the dark road, one side, then the other, as stars came out in the black sky. He checked the little metal box regularly, in case it failed to keep in The Frank, whose noise continued.

"If you must go back to that airport office like you originally planned, Christine, I'd feel better if you took Paul with you."

"I don't need a bodyguard."

"He's useful in other ways. He can help you search. Are you sure Greene didn't find what he was looking for?"

"He left in a hurry when I let him go and wasn't carrying anything. I put a few of Paul's bugs in strategic places. There have been no sounds, so Greene hasn't been back. I need to know what would make a man in his position act that way. Are you sure there's no other record of Caslander and Greene being in the same vicinity?"

"Positive, my dear, other than in Thailand thirty years ago. But Greene had no role that would put him in Caslander's orbit. He was a dependent of his wife, a secretary for Air America. He didn't even hold a job."

They stopped talking when the car entered an open space, flat and empty, dark with only starlight. Christine turned off the headlights and drove toward a low square shape darker against the sky.

Fluffy fought the temptation to curl up in his box. The noises from Christine and The Frank hadn't held any tension, only human-style communication, like a low growl or a hello bark, and it made him sleepy. There were repeated sounds, but none he recognized, and only one that he knew, which was bugs. It was a word Christine used when she put him in the sink and got his fur all wet and soapy with fowl smelling stuff.

He growled—at the word and at The Frank, who now had a freshly-earned bad association in Fluffy's mind. But at least it kept him alert so that when Christine stopped the car by the square shape and another car without lights pulled up beside them, he exploded into the fierce predator he knew he was.

22

"Sorry, Fluffbutt," said Christine, "you'll have to stay in here while I give this asshole a piece of my mind." She got out and locked the car door behind her as she turned to the nuisance, scowling at him with ready words. He beat her to it.

"Shut the dog up, Christine," said Paul. "I can hear him through the glass. What makes you think you can be clandestine carting around that appendage twenty-four-seven?"

Don't even try to explain to this guy. He has no soul. "If I were the only one out here," she said aloud through her teeth, "and if he weren't locked in the car, we'd have all the stealth we need. As it is, your presence does more to hinder than help. Who put you up to it? Frank?

"Nobody. I tailed you here. Ridiculously easy because you weren't even checking. I make only two demands on you, Christine, and I'm repeating both right now. Follow my advice when it comes to security and keep me in the loop!"

His voice was low but vehement, a hissing whisper. Fluffy threatened to drown him out. It was time to get him out of the car. She opened the passenger door and winced as the little dog launched himself to the ground, putting too much stress on that lone front shoulder. She expected him to latch onto Paul's ankle, but the fool dog greeted the man with his whole hind end wagging. Paul bent down to pet him.

Traitor.

When nobody's satisfied, it can be a mark of a successful negotiation. In this case, only one of them seemed delighted. Fluffy sat butt to tarmac, tail still wagging, tongue out and ears upright. The two humans looked at him for a long moment. Paul sighed and said, "Set your alarms, lock your car, and let's go. The night is no longer young."

He loomed over her right shoulder as Christine pulled the toolkit Paul had given her from the deep front pocket of her utility vest. The lock gave easily. She heard him grunt, probably congratulating himself on having taught her something. She tamped down a pang of gratitude.

"What are we looking for here?" he asked as he straightened.

The face of him, assuming I want his help!

"I told you this morning. Whatever Greene didn't find here," she said levelly."

He didn't reply, so she filled in the rest. "This was Caslander's center of operations for the airport. From what I read in Justin's files, airfields were a constant in his life, so… center of ops, center of life. I'm assuming the mayor's been looking for something Caslander left behind— something that damages him. I don't need your help."

I have Fluffy.

"Thanks for the explanation," he said, pushing the door open from behind. "That wasn't so hard, was it? Communication's not a bad thing. Neither is accepting help. Four eyes are better than two."

Six eyes and a nose.

She gave a slight nod, a scowling acquiescence she doubted he could appreciate in the dark. "Fluffy comes with." It was non-negotiable, and anyway, he was way ahead of them in the dark hallway. Paul turned the beam of a flashlight on the little dog, who paused at each doorway for a sniff before moving toward the larger open ops center at the end.

Christine turned on the lights in the windowless room, and in the chart room behind the counter. Paul picked up a folding chair and box of pens and headed back down the hall.

"What are you doing?" she asked.

"Setting up an alarm to warn us if somebody comes through that door," he said over his shoulder.

"We don't need that."

He stopped and turned, ready to argue. She pointed to Fluffy, busy scrabbling along the front of the counter. "We have an alarm."

A mouse headed to the chartroom seeking refuge. Fluffy was on the job. He brought his trophy and laid the poor thing at Christine's feet. She met Paul's eyes and noted his grimace.

"He is a rat terrier, Paul. You're not the only fierce hunter on the planet." She suppressed a laugh, but it came through in the brightness of her voice.

Paul put the box on the counter, the chair against a wall, and headed for the chart room. "I'll start in here," he called over his shoulder.

...

"Three hours and nothing." Paul stood over Christine as she sat cross-legged on the floor sifting through the last folder in the bottom drawer of the last file cabinet. She folded her arms over the open drawer and rested her forehead on the back of her hand.

He looked at the dog curled in her lap. Fluffy twitched with muted woofs in a doggy dream.

"I'm calling it a night, Christine. There's nothing here."

To his surprise, she agreed. Paul followed her to her place and watched as she and Fluffy opened the back door. He stayed parked outside long enough to see the upstairs lights go on before putting the truck in gear. Still fully clothed, he hit the cot in the loft of the barn they used for training.

And dreamt about a dead mouse.

23

P aul brought donuts. "You look like death not even warmed over," he said as he stepped into the office. She sat at her desk, hunched over a mug of coffee, and lifted sleepy eyes with forklift-level effort.

He shared the feeling. "Get some sugar in you. You need the energy." He placed the box in front of her and opened it. She selected a dusted jelly donut and mumbled thank you. Paul picked up a glazed and sat in a client chair.

Fluffy, who slept twenty hours a day but never seemed tired, placed his butt decisively on the floor at Paul's feet, ears erect, staring at the donut in his hand. Paul pinched a small piece and dropped it at Fluffy's feet. The dog moved like an electric current on a switch, then resumed the expectant pose. Paul had an inkling he was on to something in his relationship with the creature. He looked up to see Christine smiling faintly.

"Whaddaya say we go over Caslander's house again tonight," he said, hoping with everything in him that she would send the very thought of it into the oblivion the suggestion deserved.

"No."

She croaked the word between chews. A dusting of powdered sugar decorated her upper lip. Paul enjoyed the welcome negative and waited, wanting her to share her reasoning.

When she did, he considered this a red letter day. They were communicating. Haltingly, distantly, often at oblique if not cross purposes, but—garbled, incomplete, sketchy and scarce—information was passing between them.

"There's no point, Paul. Greene had all the time he needed to turn it over thoroughly—and he's no slouch. We saw that last night. Even though I interrupted him, the spaces he had time to get to were well-reamed." She shook her head, swishing a ponytail set higher than usual, like a schoolgirl. She continued, "He searched the airport after the house. That means he found nothing in the house. Caslander had another hiding place."

"Where?"

She shrugged, doubtful. "His car?"

"I imagine Greene got to that by now, don't you?"

She nodded as she swallowed and returned to her coffee. "It—whatever *it* is—has to be someplace the mayor would not know about or have access to. That is, if Caslander knew Greene would want it."

Paul's turn to nod. "And whatever it is, Greene wants it bad enough to assault you when you interrupt him in the heat of his search. Politicians tend to be more careful than that."

"I assaulted him, Paul."

"You said he shoved you first. That qualifies."

"My attack was more effective." She swallowed the last of her donut and the tough girl expression sweetened just a little. With the merest hint of reluctance, she said, "Thank you for showing me that move. It worked."

Yep. Definitely a red-letter day.

Paul ate a lot more of the remaining donuts, though Christine did take one other. She fed most of it to Fluffy, who came back to Paul when that well dried up.

He was on his fourth and final, with the attentive dog parked before him, when Christine leaned back in her chair and said, "So, how is sword-man coming along?"

Paul took his time swallowing. "That's a good code name for him. You should assign it, seeing as how you're in charge."

He was rewarded with a grin. Considering their dismal failure at the airport the night before and the persistent stalemate in the case, she was in far too good a mood. He wondered again about the complexity of women before answering the question.

"Joe—he'll need a game name, too—has enrolled in the local community college. Rusty set him up in an efficiency apartment, urged him to go for computer courses. I told him to go ahead. So he did."

"How do you make sure he's not triple dealing us? Are we paying him, too?"

Paul shook his head. "It's all about the relationship. I guess I remind him of Caslander. He misses him. And his dad. The dad ran out when he was seven. Also, I told him he'd be working for his people. He's strong in his identity. His mom gave him that much at least, along with the desire to escape her." He noticed Christine turn solemn, dropping her eyes to her hands on the desk. He remembered her opinion about motherhood and used it. "He loves her of course, but wants to make his own way."

That did the trick. He congratulated himself when she allowed another smile, this one soft and a little sad.

"So where should we look next?" he asked.

"What about Joe? If they were that close, maybe Caslander gave him something to keep for him."

Paul took a moment to think. "Or... hid it in Mary Catherine's house."

God, he liked her smiles. Even better than her occasional bitchiness. *Stop it. Work only. I'll be lucky if she ever forgives me.*

"She works during the day," said Christine, "and the house is screened by forest on one side."

"You're proposing a daytime mini-op?"

"Or interrogating Joseph. Which is easier?"

He nodded. "The mini-op might be, only because Joe's got a lot going on and I don't want him distracted. Anyway, are we sure he didn't kill Caslander?"

She turned her chair toward the side window and stared at the peeling paint on the privacy fence. She seemed to be reviewing things, Paul decided, like a checklist of memories. He wondered.

She turned back to him, inventory complete. "Yes, we're sure."

"It would be nice if we both knew why." It was the gentlest prod for information.

"I've talked to both of them. No, I take that back. I listened to both. Mary Catherine wants only him."

"Ewww."

She shook her head. "No, not like that, but just as potentially destructive. Maybe worse. It's emotional, not physical. All her eggs are in that basket and she expects him to deliver. It's a kind of emotional abuse. Hard to spot from the outside."

"And him?"

"He wants a future—his own future."

Paul remembered himself at that age, how the future seemed roomy and vast—too large for serious consideration when all pains and pleasures seemed close-by. "So, what he wants is a girl."

Despite Paul's recent ideological revolution, it was funny how some things hadn't changed.

24

Joe Stinson had urges. He tamped them down out of the habit of purity his mother taught him. But he was Joe now, no longer Joseph. He allowed himself an urge or two and indulged it today in a cup of coffee at the shop on Central Street, the one where he met Rusty and near the library where he met Paul.

Mom would disapprove of both men.

He drank his coffee black, because that's how Paul drank it. Paul reminded him of Lew. Rusty was more like Mom. All the secret shit from both of them confused Joe, but his gut told him to follow Paul. He went with his gut, partly because he missed Lew.

That's why he put up with the rigamarole Paul required for meeting him at an old barn in the woods, the circling back and checking for tails. It was a long walk from the bus, made longer by new rules with names like 'procedure' and 'tradecraft.'

Paul was late, as usual. Joe wondered if that was by design. He sat on a log by the door but couldn't stay there, waiting without patience; he had to move around. He had a Trig test scheduled in a few hours and an assignment due in History. Mom kept crying when he called her, and…

"Stop pacing."

Joe spun around to face Paul. Was there a back way to this barn? Had he been there all that time? He opened his mouth to ask but was cut off.

"Develop the habit of being still. You can't notice anything if you keep moving like that, no sounds, no movements, no threats. Get that under your bonnet."

The guy even talked like Lew.

"How did you get past me?"

"I just told you how. You were distracting yourself." Paul threw a plastic bottle of spring water at him. He caught it, but had no time to feel good about it before the workout began.

An hour later, the session ended with Joe panting for breath, dripping, and guzzling the last of the bottle. Paul hadn't even broken a sweat. Joe sported a few new bruises from the five-minute sparring session. But he vindicated himself at the end of it by landing a thrust kick square on the solar plexus. It didn't budge Paul, but the fact that he finally hit the guy exhilarated him.

They sat on a bench at the side of the mat. Paul wiped his face with his towel and took a long drink from his water bottle. "So how's you're new place? Getting settled in?"

"I guess." *How to explain it?*

"What's wrong?"

"You mean besides all the shit I don't understand? I don't even know where to start asking questions."

"Not that," said Paul after the last gulp from his water bottle. "That will come in time. There's something else bothering you."

He threw the empty bottle on the floor behind the bench. Mom would be appalled. She would make him pick it up. The act disturbed and delighted Joe at the same time.

Paul gave him another verbal nudge. "Tell me."

Joe sighed, dropped his chin to his chest to avoid eye contact. "I feel guilty leaving Mom. The more I like my place, the more I feel guilty. When she calls, I can hear it in her voice that she needs me, even when she doesn't actually say it. She wants to quit her job. Sometimes she cries. I don't know how to help her without moving back home." *He's probably thinking I'm a weak-ass kid.*

"Does Rusty know about this?"

Paul sounded serious, like he took Joe serious, like Joe maybe wasn't a disappointment. "I don't think so," he said, looking up.

"He hasn't asked? Or you haven't told him?"

"Both." Joe paused in a fresh understanding, showing Paul the dawn of it with widening eyes. "Rusty makes me feel guilty, too. He's doing so much for, me but I know he expects a return."

Paul tilted his head toward him with a confidential air. "I expect a return, too, you know."

"Yeah, I get that. But there's a difference between wanting to and having to." When Paul wrinkled his brow at this, Joe tried to explain a little more. "You don't keep on reminding me I owe you."

"Did Lew want pay back?"

Joe shook his head. "I don't think so. Except maybe my good opinion with Mom, and that came natural. I was sorry when she dumped him. Sorry for both of them. She needs a man in her life."

Other than me.

"What all did he do for you?"

"Pretty much the same things Rusty's doing, except he didn't pay for an apartment. He found me that job the cops got me fired from, and he paid for the first semester at college. I was all signed up already when Rusty offered. I let him pay for next semester."

Paul stood up and picked up his workout bag, signaling End Of Session. Joe was grateful for the reminder. He would have to rush. Maybe Paul would give him a ride.

"C'mon. I'll drive you to school."

They were parked at the entrance to the Math building and Joe's hand was on the door handle before Paul spoke again. It was yet another thing like Lew, a thing Joe admired about both men. The silence.

Paul spoke as he opened the door. "So Lew never asked you for anything?"

Joe paused. "There was one time...."

25

"Bingo!" Paul said as he pushed the office door open. Christine looked up from a notebook holding the latest printout from Justin. It was the very word she had been thinking. There would be much to talk about. He rarely looked this animated.

"You first," she said. Her discovery could wait.

"Joe gave Caslander a key to his mother's house when he asked for it. The kid didn't question it and saw no sign he ever used it."

Paul lowered himself into a client chair with measured grace, his eyes on her, his agitation only evident in the lack of a coffee mug in his hand. That he would delay his habitual necessity meant something.

She had to tease. "My turn. Greene told a big lie during his first campaign for mayor. He co-opted Caslander's record at Air America as his own. It's on video and mentioned repeatedly by his many admirers—and voters—in print, and during elections. He has ambitions."

Paul's index finger tapped the arm of the chair.

A nervous gesture? It's not like him.

"It goes to motive," she added.

The tapping became faster. Christine held back her impatience. The man wanted something.

"When does Caslander's girlfriend go to work?" he said.

She took a moment to reply while he stood and headed to the coffee machine.

"You want to do this in daylight?" She couldn't hide the surprise in her voice.

"You're telling me she's at her bank right now? Let's go, then."

Risky. But she had come to appreciate the predatory nature of a hunter. He was focused and alert, all his senses pointing in one direction. He scented more than possibility. She had to respect that. After all, she respected Fluffy.

"Okay," she said. "We'll take your truck. My Jeep has been there too many times." She retrieved Fluffy's collar and harness from a hook on the door.

"We're not taking the dog."

"Oh yes we are, Paul."

"He doesn't fit this time. He's too noticeable, especially with two people moving through brush on the river bank to sneak in through a back door or window. We will have to move quickly—freely."

Christine took a semi-deep breath, allowed her gaze to tell him she wasn't just throwing words at him. He was right to be intense, and the argument made sense. She glanced at Fluffy. His tail was up, his stance also intense. Did they know they resembled each other in this moment? It didn't matter—*she* knew.

"I admit you're right, Paul. But we're taking him. Blame instinct."

Both mine and Fluffy's.

She watched the war going on in his eyes. Nothing in his expression moved; no muscle twitched. Typical White man, she thought. He believes his only role on earth is as predator. Every other animal lives as both predator and prey. He is unaware even vegetarian foragers have deadly defenses.

How do I show him how connected everything is? Do I care enough to try?

The answer was no. She owed him nothing. Why the six months he spent foraging for survival in a forest taught him so little was a mystery and not her problem. Maybe it converted him from a racist ass, but it didn't affect his view of all the planetary others he must have encountered while he scrambled to exist. That was his loss.

And besides, I still don't trust him.

The internal war going on behind Paul's blue eyes ended with a white flag. He swallowed more coffee, put the hot mug down on her desk—*another deficit in his training*—and pulled out his keys. "Let's go then," he said.

Okay. He might be teachable, but now there was a heat ring in the finish of her new desk.

26

Everything delighted Fluffy. He didn't care that his whole body told on him. He zoomed. He spun. His tail did helicopter twirls. He barked, high and piercing, until both humans shouted, "Stop it!"

Because it was a chorus of shouts that mixed with his own, he considered it a sign of agreement. He paused only when his beloved one opened the wrong door on the wrong car, the one that smelled of rotted french fries under the seats.

"Get in," she said.

Fluffy knew those words. It added joy to an already joyous occasion. Any time he got to ride in the human-mobile was by definition good. Unless it took him to the vet. But that wasn't likely. He remembered the last time. There were needles. They never went there when he still remembered needles. Smells and foreboding, yes. Needles, no.

They stopped at a traffic light. Christine held him in her lap as he pressed his nose on the window beside her. A big truck pulled alongside, its engine thrumming over the sound of the little truck they were in. He looked up, saw the man in the big truck looking down at him—at Christine—and bared his teeth. He snarled. Christine patted him, rewarding his prowess at protecting her.

The little truck moved on. The humans made their usual noises. Fluffy attached significance to some sounds, like dinner and walk, but for the most part allowed the music of Christine's voice to give him a feeling of well-being. He continually scanned all other noises for signs of threat or emergency.

"You want to explain to me why the mutt has to go everywhere with you?" said Paul.

Fluffy turned away from his minute inspection of the traffic ahead to look at him. It had sounded like a growl.

"No."

Fluffy knew this word, but it was not directed at him. He went back to watching traffic.

"I get it," said Paul. "You don't owe me any explanations. But when you're working with somebody, it's good policy to stay in touch, to brief each other. You never know. A little knowledge can save lives. In an emergency, our brains sift through a bunch of unrelated shit. It can make a difference if one little piece of what we oughta know isn't there."

The growling had stopped and there was no more traffic. Fluffy elected to take a nap, curling himself on Christine's lap. Her voice was calm and soothing.

"Okay Paul. If one little piece of information can make a difference, as you say, why limit it?"

"Huh?"

"Why limit information to just human sources?"

"I don't follow you."

"I'm answering your question about why I take him everywhere. Besides the bond that keeps me balanced, he provides information. I don't understand how you could have spent six months in the forest without catching on to it."

Paul stopped for a red light and turned to stare at her. "Catching on to what?"

"To sources of information all around you."

"In a forest?"

"Precisely."

"I was alone! You have no idea what you're...."

A car behind them blared its horn. Fluffy looked up, knowing it was a sign of human incompetence to make such noises. They had weak voices.

The voices of the humans he was riding with became silent. He wanted to go back to his nap, but something was wrong. Fluffy felt tension and smelt hostility.

...

Christine nearly tripped over Fluffy. The dog had become more watchful, swinging his ears from side to side, bringing those big ears to bear on the forest that crowded the path. He should be enjoying the walk, she thought, the scent of the river, the sounds of animals staying out of his way.

"Can't you keep him on your other side?" asked Paul. "I nearly kicked him twice now."

"I don't know what's wrong with him," she said. "He senses something."

"In the forest?"

"Or in us."

The length of time it took for Paul to comment again told Christine much. He was angry. At her? At Fluffy? At life in general?

She stopped. The unseen river gurgled behind undergrowth on their right. Fluffy, ever in tune with every nuance of Christine's movement, plopped his butt on the ground next to her left foot, ears up, nose pointed at Paul, his canines visible.

Paul stopped after another pace. He turned, snorted, and gave an exasperated sigh. "What the hell is it now?" he said.

"Look at Fluffy." The dog's explanation was pretty clear.

"What?"

"Look at him. What do you see?"

"Is he snarling? There's no sound, but his teeth are showing."

"Because, over all, he likes you."

"Funny way to show it." Paul's voice had gravel in it, like a growl. Fluffy let out a little of his own warning noise.

"If he didn't like you, he'd be attacking right now." Christine made an effort to relax her stance, trusting Fluffy's assessment of the man, a lesson she learned about her dog long ago. It was Paul's turn to learn these things. She did not relish the role of teacher and hoped the man would listen to Fluffy.

"Why the fuck would he attack me?"

His f-word was too vehement. Fluffy's growl became audible.

"He's warning you," she said, keeping her voice even and low. "Fluffy knows you're angry. He does not trust angry men. He doesn't trust anybody who might hurt me." She concentrated on her next breath, reminding herself that sometimes teachable moments come at inconvenient times.

"So?" Again, the sound of belligerence.

"So say it. Why are you angry?"

His face, normally so controlled, minimally betrayed an emotion. Not anger. More like a man at the edge of a chasm, about to step off, wondering who packed the parachute on his back. Revolutions happen in these small moments.

"I'm not," he said slowly, squinting one eye. "I was. But I'm not. Not angry. Trust me. That's all I'm asking for. Some sign of your trust."

...

Fluffy was able to enjoy the smell of the small prey rustling the brush nearby because all was well. The humans made their sounds and inexplicably the tension eased. He would have liked to investigate it, but they moved on and he had to run point, to clear any hazards before them.

They left the trees and approached a doorway facing the river. The Paul opened it, using those nimble human fingers holding a metal stick. Fluffy was disappointed. Human dens tended to be uninteresting, a good place to sleep—one of his favorite occupations—but devoid of good smells. This place didn't even have a cat.... He made himself comfortable on a soft chair near Christine and closed his eyes.

But wait.... His nose hinted at it, then a sound came to his ears. His body tensed and the nose pointed, giving him the full scent and the chase was on.

Fluffy emerged victorious. Of course. He never had any doubt. When Christine pried his trophy from his teeth, he felt no resentment, only satisfaction that once again, he had proved his value to his pack.

27

P aul saw it. It wasn't obvious at first, but the dog's clicking toenails, scrambling and sliding over the bare wood floor caught his attention. He stopped trying to pry open the hilt of a very fine saber he had taken from the wall. Anyway, it looked like one piece and would probably require smashing.

Desperation had made made him try the swords on the wall. Christine was busy with the cushions of the couch, searching for signs of a hand-sewn seam. Not that either one of them thought Caslander would have been capable of bringing a sewing kit when he stashed whatever it was he had hidden here.

They both knew, in their bones, almost like a bonding moment between them, this was the place.

And after forty diligent, creative minutes, they found nothing.

Christine ruled out slicing open soft furniture or busting walls. Paul was disappointed but getting used to letting her be the boss. There would come a time when he would know she was wrong, and then…. In the meantime, he waited for further proof she was probably right while the all-important and alert pooch snored in a chair

Not a lot of information coming from there.

No more than thirty seconds after the last thought, Fluffy launched his muscular little body at the wall, scrabbled along the baseboard. He emerged in triumph, delighted with his victory and unwilling to give up the trophy. Christine had to force open his jaws to remove the poor, dead furry thing. She held it by the tail at arm's length, expecting Paul to do the manly and dispose of it.

Dream on. Paul stared unseeing at the baseboard behind the scene of Fluffy's conquest. A small dime-sized spot of blood glistened next to the wall.

"I saw paper towels in the kitchen," Christine said, still holding up the body.

Next step will be to convert the hint into an order. But he couldn't stop staring at that wall.

Fluffy was making mighty leaps to reclaim it. Christine raised her arm higher.

For once in their so-called collaboration, Paul knew not to be distracted from what he knew—he just knew—he needed to do. The thing, whatever it was, had been hidden here, in this house, this room. The blood on the floor was significant. Why? Was it mouse blood? Was it missed by the crime-scene cleaner? *No way. They wouldn't miss anything.* What made him stand staring at it?

Am I turning into some kind of mystic?

Paul softened his gaze, expanding it around that circle of blood, a centimeter at a time, and there it was. A crack in the baseboard, a separation from the wall. and a light spot behind and under.

Christine was clearing her throat. She grimaced as the mouse body dangled from her fingers.

Paul crossed the floor and knelt before the wall, inspecting the blood. It was fresh and belonged to the late mouse. He fit one finger behind the loose baseboard and pulled gently, then used thumb and finger of the other hand to grasp the corner of lightweight blue paper firmly enough to bring it out of its hiding place intact.

28

"What's it say?" Paul pressed the accelerator to beat the fresh yellow light ahead. He glanced at her as she folded the letter and put it in an outside compartment of her carrier bag. Fluffy lay inside it, audibly snoring. The dog could sleep anywhere.

She didn't answer.

Paul scowled and snorted, exasperated. "The dog did nothing special, you know, Christine. There's no mystical Indian magical power here that made us find that paper because he killed a mouse. So what is it? A note? A letter?" *When is the damn woman going to include me?*

"The term to use is Native American and I never said Fluffy was magical."

He had to admit, only to himself, a twinge of relief that she was at least talking.

"You didn't say it, but you're thinking it."

"No. I'm not. You misunderstood me. I didn't insist we bring him because of any superpower. He's a dog. He acted like a dog and did what he thought was important to do. That's all he did. But we would not have found that letter if he didn't. When you're a team, each member brings something."

"Team?" Paul had always been solo, fighting God's war alone or as an independent adjunct to others, until a former enemy team brought him down—way down—and until he surfaced again on the other side, gasping for understanding. He took the I-95 exit ramp at Union Street and turned the truck toward Christine's office.

"Sounds like airy-fairy Native American mystical shit to me," he said. "You must have learned it from your folks."

She spoke again after a noisy sigh. She was about to spill, he realized, and it made him patient, stripped away the urge for a fight. He concentrated on listening.

"I grew up mostly in foster care, Paul. When I was allowed to be with my family, it was never long enough to absorb all their culture or any more than bare competence in the language. But I remember my grandfather telling me about the animals and the plants, telling me to watch and listen. I am ashamed to say I thought he was crazy. It was much later when I found out he wasn't. Do you want to hear it?"

"You know I do."

She paused, maybe regretting the offer of actual information. He glanced sideways. She was staring straight ahead.

"When I was a rookie state trooper, my shift was tasked to help with a stakeout in support of the Mounties over the border. They were tracking a clandestine shipment of guns on its way through Vermont to Canada. Some of us were in pairs, others by themselves. I was placed in an an unmarked car, alone, in the brush off a dirt road and told to stay off the radio and just watch for any activity. I brought a large thermos of coffee and sat there all night, amazed at the drama going on all around me." She stopped and looked at him until his glance told her to go on.

"That's how bored I was. Everybody came through there, deer, opossums, rabbits, foxes, coyotes, voles, fisher cats, even a bull moose and a mama bear with two cubs. A nature-lover's dream."

"So, you got in touch with your inner Ind… Native American."

"No. I just wanted to go home. All those animals were going about their business, waking up, hunting, foraging, evading predators—I could tell after a while—digging nests and going to sleep. I desperately wanted to do the same. Then everything changed."

"How so?" Paul had to admit to himself he wanted to know.

"Every animal in my sight vanished into the brush and no new ones came through the little clearing. The neighborhood was eerily empty. The sky had cleared and the moon was even brighter than it had been, but I figured it couldn't be the extra light that made them avoid the place. It only gave them, and me, a wider circle of vision. It took me too much time, but I finally decided they must be hiding. I suspected I should, too."

"And?"

"I took the animals' advice, got out of the car, locked it, found a thick patch of undergrowth, dragged a branch over where I had stepped, like in the movies, and watched the road from there. No more than five minutes later, here comes a big black pickup, lights out. It didn't stop as it passed my car, though they should have seen it."

"Still," said Paul, "it was good thinking to take evasive action. I wonder why they didn't check."

"They knew I was there, Paul. I told dispatch. They copied. That's the last I ever heard about the case."

He cogitated silently. That's the word his grandpa would use. *Link your thoughts, boy, seek the pathways to understanding.* Of course, Gramps often found a pathway to culpability in somebody with too much melanin. Funny how prejudice becomes the link in a chain of thought that skews results.

Paul consciously threw away his preconceptions, good and bad, about law enforcement. "The smugglers had a mole in your organization, or in the Mounties."

"It had to be mine. The Mounties would not have known anything about our details."

"And they picked you because you were a rookie? Or because you're a woman?"

"You forgot Native American. Yes. All the above. But I made lieutenant eventually, so it's all good, right?"

Paul parked under the overhang behind her building and turned off the ignition before he realized she still had not shared what he was sure was a letter. He recognized a corner of the old-fashioned light-weight airmail paper in her bag.

Some team. It took his mind a solid minute to process all these new thoughts. The engine ticked as it cooled.

When he turned to look at her, she smiled. "Fluffy thinks his role on my team is to protect me—against anything that moves. The only magic about this letter is that Fluffy did his job and we did ours, and without his dead mouse and your sharp eyes, we would not have found this." She held up the paper. "It's the magic of teams, Paul. Fluffy has my back and I have his."

Is she saying I'm on this team? Who has my back?

She was out of the car and on her way to the door. He hurried to catch up, neglecting to set his alarms, but in time to see hers. She saw him notice. A slight nod. She had let him see her alarms.

I'm on this team. Me and the dog.

It was the first sign of trust and it both thrilled him and filled him with uncomfortable questions. He had betrayed his previous loyalties, discarded a world view he now considered obnoxious and dangerous. He could not go back, not only because they all wanted him dead, but because he could not unsee how much of it was a lie.

Christine tilted her head toward the coffee machine. He was on a team headed by a woman who was firmly in charge. He and a ten-pound rat terrier. He made coffee. As it began to gurgle, she handed him the paper they had pulled from behind a baseboard. *They*—whichever one of them did the pulling was immaterial.

I'm not _on_ the team. I belong to it. Just like the dog.

29

"**S**o does this mean you trust me now?"

Paul lifted one side of his mouth in sarcastic skepticism.

Christine frowned at it. *He tries my patience.* Why the hell did he think he rated any confidence at all? She remembered the bruises last year and deepened her scowl. He missed the frown as he read the hasty scrawl on airmail paper. It took only a moment.

"Who is Vivian?" he asked.

Paul's blue eyes would have looked innocent if she hadn't met another guy with similar eyes in charge of the people supporting her mission. Blue eyes can be cold, too, she reminded herself.

He had more questions. "Why don't you ask Justin, boss lady? Or did you do that already?"

His puffy-cheeked chipmunk smile was almost endearing, and there was minimally more respect than sarcasm in 'boss lady'. Christine took a moment to give herself permission to be a little reckless.

"Why don't you ask him, Paul?"

He had the sense not to goad the future or lament the past, but couldn't hide his shock at this mark of trust. Not that she couldn't change the password as soon as he was done. And the web address would not lead to Justin's location. Even she didn't know where that was, and Paul was no hacker.

She rolled her chair aside to give him room, lifting her chin to indicate the computer on the credenza. "His web address is on the pink notepad next to the keyboard. Password is ericdied, all lower case, one word."

"That's not secure—more like an invitation than a password."

"You think it's safe to try to hack Justin?"

Paul pursed his lips. "Good point." He pulled a small chair from the corner and sat before the computer. "What, exactly, do we want to know—I mean, besides who the hell is Vivian?"

"Do you remember if we've seen that name in all the other printouts Justin sent?" Christine stepped over to the counter to refill her cup. "There's one more cup in here, Paul. Do you want it?" He nodded toward his mug. She brought the pot and poured before sitting down next to him.

"Thanks," he said. "I remember the name. Greene was married to a Vivian."

Married. Her memory flashed one snippet of conversation in the long litany she had endured with Frank. "Treat it like a marriage," Christine remembered him saying. "Give him time and he'll come around. You'll get used to each other." Frank rolled his bulging eyes at her stony silence. "Of course, it's plat... celib—there's no sex, Christine. You know damn well I didn't mean that." Then he launched an interrogation into her working relationships in the state police. Wasn't she close to her fellow troopers?

No. I was too female for them.

You faced tough situations together?

Yes, and they blamed me for being female.

Get together for a beer occasionally?

No, I had a child to raise. Christine's son never went to foster care.

Frank got the hint after she inflicted more silence. "All I'm saying is treat him like a partner. Assume he can figure things out."

In other words, don't nag.

Christine watched as Paul stared at the blinking cursor. She did her best to practice self control, tried to relax into it. The effort made one eye twitch. Her mouth opened, ready to deliver biting words, when he lifted his hand to the keyboard and using just one index finger, laboriously typed the web address of Justin.

Then the password.

Her eye twitched again as he formulated a question, then swung his head to her as Justin's answer came to the screen. "How the hell does this guy know it's not you asking? Are we under surveillance?"

"Frank sweeps every time he's here," Christine said, shaking her head. "I wouldn't put it past them, but I haven't found anything. Maybe he knows it's not me because you took so much time typing the question."

"So? I majored in knife-fighting in high school. They only put girls in front of typewriters." He turned back to the screen. "Justin wants to know who I am."

Where did I put that old Typing Tutor floppy disk?

She didn't think she should have to say anything and was unwilling to torture herself by watching him hunt and peck over the keyboard, so she made another pot of coffee, then took Fluffy out the back door to his favorite grassy patch of weeds. When they came back inside, the printer was spitting out twenty-five pages on the life—and death—of Vivian Greene.

They each took a section of printer paper, divided at a convenient stopping point somewhere near the middle, and swapped sections after a cursory speed read. Fluffy whined.

"I thought you just took him out," said Paul.

"I did. He wants us to know—wants you to know—we better take him with us."

"Yeah. Tell him I've become resigned to it."

30

Century-old houses marched downhill in two crooked lines on either side of a potholed street. City trash cans occupied the curbs, the street near the curbs, the broken sidewalk on one side, the gutter on the other. It was trash day in this neighborhood and the truck had just come through. Not everything made it into its maw. Escaped plastic bags, aluminum cans, and bright broken toys gathered on storm drain grates.

Paul pointed to a house on the right, the downhill side of the street, where properties sloped almost vertically to a slow stream through stands of invasive Norway maple trees. Backyards behind the houses on the left were equally steep, but stretched uphill, their back fences standing as high as upstairs eaves.

Fluffy lifted his head and sat up in Paul's lap as Christine pulled the Jeep to the right, parking it behind a small pickup with a pile of brush in the bed. Paul shifted the mutt's front leg before it could cause him damage. The dog weighed only ten pounds, but it seemed all his weight came to a painful point under that tiny foot. Fluffy rose on his hind legs to put his front foot on the door. He inspected the destination, ears on high alert. He did this at every traffic light. Paul put his hand on the door latch.

"Wait," said Christine. "What exactly are we after here?"

"We need to know why he made himself a nuisance claiming his wife was murdered—to the point that police charged him with wasting their time."

Paul looked at the debris-strewn front of the house. A wrecked car leaned against a side porch. Beside it, another old car stood on cement blocks with a pair of legs in greasy jeans stretching from underneath it across the short driveway. Piles of firewood and scrap, none of it stacked, straggled down the slope to the leaning back fence.

"You know, Christine, this is not the kind of place that matches the woman I read about in 'life of Vivian.' Would she marry this after ditching the mayor? Maybe it wasn't murder. Maybe it was suicide."

Christine stifled a guffaw.

I made her laugh. He smiled.

"Lower your window a little," she said. "We'll leave Fluffy in here, but we can't be long. Now that the rain's done, it'll get hot soon."

"Just for my information, why is he not essential this time?"

"He'd only get in trouble in this junkyard."

Fluffy objected loudly, his voice muffled by the glass. Paul gave him a sympathetic glance, remembering his own experience in Montreal. *Quit your bellyaching, pooch. At least you're not lying trussed up in a pool of somebody else's blood covered in flies, hollering into a radio nobody monitors.* He freed a mint from a roll in his pocket and held it over the edge of the slightly open window. Fluffy couldn't reach it, but he saw and signaled ready, catching it easily when Paul let go. It's our secret, thought Paul. Christine was particular about her dog's diet, but she wasn't looking.

She was standing beside the greasy-jeaned legs when he reached her.

"Mr. Walker?" she said.

"Who the fuck wants to know, lady?" The voice was accompanied by a clanging sound, both voice and clang coming from under the elevated car on blocks.

Paul intervened, pitching his voice a tone lower than normal, hoping to sound bigger than he was, though he wasn't what he'd call puny, either. "We're from Barton and Company Investigations and are hoping you can fill in a little background for us on a divorce matter for a client we're helping." Christine frowned at the words 'and Company' but held it back when the man slid out from under the car.

Walker stood an inch or two taller than Paul, beefy but soft like bread dough. Paul would have no problem if things became... difficult. The man wiped grease off his hands onto the flannel shirt he wore, sleeveless and open over a black t-shirt. He was at least sixty, unfriendly and curling a lip at Christine, one eye squinted with distaste.

She kept it steady—like she did in Montreal. All strength and beauty, with burnished copper skin smooth over high cheek bones and that steady, intelligent gaze from deep brown, slightly angled eyes that saw right through you into your rotted essence. It was the look that revolutionized Paul's life. *If you know what's good for you, buddy, you'll pay attention here.* He doubted the man paid attention, but at least he answered their questions about the late Vivian Walker, the former Mrs. Greene.

"I'm telling you," Walker said, getting into his stride in the conversation, "that there line was nicked. It was a slow leak. There weren't nobody on the road and it was dry. She didn't even hit the pole with any what you'd call speed. There was no skid mark. Cops said maybe she committed suicide, drove into it deliberate, in broad daylight. I said no way. We were happy."

"They thought it was suicide but charged you with her death?" asked Christine.

"Yeah. Wicked weird, right? I'm the one who told them in the first place about the nick in the steering fluid line. I know about this shit. I was there when they winched up the car and I saw the fluid." He gestured to small puddles of drying rain on the road next to them to illustrate. "I knew it wasn't right. And if that wasn't right, what else wasn't? There was a trail of fluid spots on the road before she hit that pole. So I told them and they fuckin' arrested me! Lawyer told them to shove it. No evidence I did it. Why would I point it out to them if I did?"

"Why'd you go to the press?" asked Paul. He didn't think it much of a self-preservation move after a close call with police and could not hide his doubt about this guy.

The guy returned doubt with belligerence, pushing his chin low and forward at Paul. "Because I knew I didn't do it, but somebody else did, mister. She was my wife."

"Did it help? That was ten years ago. Did you find out anything else?"

Walker shook his head and pushed a long strand of curling grey hair behind his ear.

"The well was dry," he said, then hesitated, peering at each of them in a silence that highlighted the muffled howling escaping through the crack in Christine's Jeep window. Sorrow, loss, despair, said the howl. Walker's face and shoulders fell with each note.

"I know who did it," he said quietly. "Always knew. It wasn't anything I learned afterwards that told me. It was before—from her."

They waited, not breathing. The howling stopped. Paul wondered briefly if the heat had mounted in the car and debated going to check on Fluffy, but then the guy spoke again after a deep, breathy sigh and shuffle of his sneakers on the broken asphalt of his driveway.

"I didn't pay no attention when she told me her divorce was shitty and the court said she couldn't talk about it. Gag order, it's called. She didn't tell me, not even in confidence, like. I read it when I went through her effects and I found the decree."

"And?" said Christine, softly.

He smiled at her for the first time—almost friendly.

"And… I still got it. You want it?"

"Why should I want it?"

"Because the order was almost expired. It was gonna be up a week after she died, three weeks before the election, the first one her ex was running in."

31

J oe moved in fear, the nameless kind. Even though these guys—on both sides—called it a game, something whispered at him in the dark, even on a sunny day, that he didn't know the rules.

He doubled back as taught, slipped into shop doorways, watched reflections on windows, made multiple right turns, got on wrong buses, got off suddenly, walked to random stops, crashed through brush under the trees, stopping every so often to listen for other crashing, and arrived at the barn late.

Paul did not look pleased. "What the hell is going on, Joe?"

"I wish I knew."

Paul tilted his head and sighed as he secured the door behind them. "Tell me."

How? Joe took a breath. "Rusty found a bug in his car."

"And?"

"And why would the government bug a Canadian, Paul?"

"What makes you think it was the government? Whose government? And the jargon is tap or touch."

Joe's face registered his growing confusion. It was all so matter of fact. And anyway, what side of this 'game' was Paul on? For that matter, what side was *he* on? *Who?* and *Why?* crowded out speech. His open mouth made only beginning W sounds.

Paul waited, patient and bemused, while Joe formed a first sentence. It led to others.

"He showed it to me, Rusty did." Joe formed a circle with thumb and forefinger to illustrate. "He asked did I know who could have put it in his car. I shook my head, wondering if he was accusing me, and guess what he said." Joe opened his eyes wide, eyebrows high, as he gave Paul enough time to answer the impossible.

"What did he say?"

"He said he knew it wasn't me, because it could only have been put there while I was in class. He said he checked that I was in class. How could he do that, Paul? Am I being watched and who by? I don't know nothing, but it's creepy."

"Why?"

Joe hesitated, mouth open, breath stuck in his throat. *How can he not see how fucking creepy this is?* Better words came after he weeded out the expletives. "Because I don't know who is who, Paul. I like you. I trust you, because you're like Lew and I miss him, but you could be false, too."

Paul tilted his head to one side. "What do you mean, *too*?"

"Rusty's a fake. I can't say why I know, I just do. He kept talking about the Maine Adversary. Does Maine have some kind of Office of Adversary? What the hell?"

Joe felt relieved when Paul bit his lower lip and dipped his head to keep from laughing, like he found it absurd, too.

"He means main without the 'e', Joe. Main adversary is how he refers to the US."

"I thought Canada was friendly."

"He's not Canadian."

"He talks like it. So you know him?"

"We met briefly last year in Montreal. I thought he was Canadian, too. But now I understand he's not. Did he press you hard? Did you tell him about me?"

"He did and no, I didn't." Exasperated, Joe added, "Am I working for the White Man, Paul? I thought I was doing this for the tribe."

"Tribes, Joe. Once you're trained and in place, you'll help track threats to all the tribes, the Wabanaki Alliance and beyond. Christine is setting it up and you're in on the ground floor. It's important that you pay attention and be careful with Rusty. He's dangerous."

Joe stared at him for a long moment. "So... if I'm working for the tribes, who's Rusty working for? White supremacists or something?"

"He uses them as allies, sure, but when I met him, he told me I could refer to him as Slava, so he could be Russian."

"But you don't know? Then, you can't be working for Uncle Sam."

"That's right, I'm not. Stop thinking everything is binary, Joe. I'm your ally. You can trust that much."

Joe smiled with sudden revelation. "You're Christine's boyfriend, aren't you?"

The vehement denial and subsequent lecture on business relationships and social interaction in the workplace were too over the top to be believable, but Joe took it all on board dutifully, because he had a reason to.

He proceeded to tell Paul all about his reason. With enthusiasm.

32

C hristine sat in the corner easy chair facing the office door, Fluffy asleep beside her, snoring. She pored over a ring binder filled with only the most important pages culled from individual volumes covering the people she found interesting in the death of Lew Caslander.

Despite the danger of disregarding large parts of the information available, she put this condensed volume together because she needed a core, a memorizable synopsis of what she knew. One sheet covered bare facts about the ancillaries, people she had interviewed, those with firm alibis, known troublemakers on the largely peaceful island reservation, and petty criminals in Old Town on the river bank that even the police had rejected as possibles.

It wasn't a robbery. It was somebody capable of lifting an antique Crusader sword. The crime seemed motiveless. Self defense? Or, did Mary Catherine have another boyfriend?

"Ah, sex!" said Paul as he came through the door.

Fluffy picked up his head, blinked, and tucked his nose back under his paw.

"Don't goad me, Paul."

"What's with the dog? He's not even growling at me."

"He's used to you. What about sex?"

"Interesting proposition, I'm flattered. But this is not that kind of relationship, you know. Strictly business, you and me. Besides, I haven't cleaned up yet after my workout with Joe. There's no shower in that old barn and I had to spend extra time dry cleaning the way back. The kid's nervous."

He pulled a client chair over to face her and plonked down into it, sweat still sticking hair to his forehead.

"You had quite a workout," she said. "I can tell by the smell. You brought up sex, first thing in the door. Why?"

They regarded each other eye to eye, but not mind to mind, though Christine had to admit a certain amount of mutual speculation and curiosity might be in the air. She certainly felt it. Maybe the t-shirt he wore hugged his biceps too well.

She looked away before he answered.

"Rusty is introducing a woman to Joe. She'll be his controller. Old, according to Joe, at least thirty, but built. Also according to him."

And he wasn't referring to biceps. Christine smiled at the irony. "You think he'll fall in love and blow our network of one?"

"Three. And Fluffy makes four. I'll remind you again about that bone-headed move of interviewing Joe while he sat behind you. Fluffy was in his car seat. Joe knows your weakness."

"Maybe Rusty's tired of the drive. He's based in Montreal. Has Joe met this new controller?" She hesitated and corrected herself. "Of course he did, if he's measured her charms already."

This got her a full-on grin. "No, Rusty showed him a picture.That's the bad news. He's already pretty smitten. The good news is Rusty's spooked. He'll be spending more time in Montreal. We can make progress with Joe only if he can keep his brain out of his pants."

"He's what? Twenty-two years old? What are the chances of that, and why is Rusty spooked?" She propped the binder on the floor against the chair, contemplating coffee. She stood and stepped toward the counter.

"I saw his car parked at his favorite hotel yesterday, so I knew he's in town and thought it would be interesting to try a light touch on the car. It didn't work; he found it right away, but he brought it up with the kid and I think that's why he's setting up a cut-out controller. He's been spooked. I think we need to talk to Frank. Do you mind if I use your shower upstairs to clean up?"

"You're always complaining about communication, Paul. You know it goes both ways." Christine scowled at him through lowered eyebrows. "You should have cleared the touch with me first."

"I know. I'm sorry—but about Frank, can I clean up before you call him?"

"No need to call him, but yes, go clean up. We're meeting him at the airport in an hour.

33

Fluffy adored car rides. The Paul could growl all he wanted; it would not spoil his joy. There were too many threatening but interesting things to be alert to. His tail betrayed emotion; excitement ruled, and Fluffy drank it in thirstily.

It was true Christine was calm, steady, herself of perfection as always. The excitement came to his tail by way of The Paul. Despite the occasional growl from the man when he stood up in his lap, Fluffy could smell concern and anticipation.

The only less than wonderful part of this ride was the sound of the dreaded word. The Beloved Christine and The Paul both said the word frank too many times. So many, in fact, that Fluffy stopped growling every time he heard it. Maybe this was a training session, but if it was, where were the treats? Whoever heard of training without treats?

"Where are we meeting him?" asked Paul.

"In the FBO at the airport."

"Not the terminal?"

The car stopped in the left turn lane behind a red light. A semi stopped to the right and the driver made faces at Fluffy, who acknowledged and engaged with all his might, jumping at the glass and causing The Paul to make loud sounds that he knew meant *stop it*. But he couldn't.

Fluffy led the way into the building, straining the leash, nose ready, voice at full volume, through the door, slipping on the floor, toenails scraping for purchase, the first molecules of that scent reaching a memory center. An unpleasant one.

He sat abruptly, gathered his dignity, and showed The Frank his teeth.

...

Paul stared at the tall Asian man introduced as Skosh standing next to Frank. He remembered the terror that consumed him last year as he ran from the Montreal disaster. This man stopped him and replied only "deep state" when Paul asked him who he was.

So I'm right about Rusty. But I thought the Cold War was over.

He forced himself to address Frank. "We could use some suggestions...."

Frank turned to Christine without replying. "How goes the investigation?"

"We know who did it," she said.

Paul tried to add, "But we can't prove it...." But he stopped again when the deep state guy raised his chin toward him and asked Christine, "Are you vouching for him now?"

She nodded. A bit slowly, to Paul's taste. He tried to hide his discomfort with present company and the lukewarm endorsement from Christine, by saying, "Do you know....?" But Frank held up one hand.

"Not here. Not secure." Then with a sigh, Frank turned and gestured that they should follow him through air so full of suspicion even Fluffy muted his presence as Paul and his ten-pound teammate walked behind Christine out onto the ramp. The big guy lurked in the rear. She picked up her dog to climb the steps into a biggish biz-jet sitting there. Paul came next into the large cabin and knew—just knew—he owed his life not to the blue-eyed older guy who didn't shoot him when he should have, nor to the younger one who pulled him up out of the dust after that knife fight in Montreal. As he surveyed the hard gazes of three other armed men and a blonde woman wearing a Glock, he realized the process of redemption had been both sudden and gradual, intentional and accidental, but the culmination of his survival happened only a few moments before when Christine nodded.

She vouched for me.

...

Christine took the seat Mack pointed to, on his right. *They're still criminals.* Fluffy whined from her lap. Charlie, Mack's son, smiled at her—*smiled!*—and asked how she was. *Please don't be nice to me. I prefer to despise you.*

They sat poor Paul between Sergei and Steve. Funny how he was now poor Paul. Last year, he was the enemy. She looked at him, at the three of them sitting in a row across from her. Hard men, smarter, more sane and fit than her homicidal ex, but equally capable of criminality, albeit in a good cause, a cause Paul had fought against only last year.

What do I know about him that allows me to trust him? She reviewed a short history and a few words. He had survived alone in a forest, examining his own soul, patching it with intentions approved by Frank, who sat two seats to the left and across from Rimas, who smiled at her with a twinkle. Frank grinned at Paul. *So Frank trusts him.* But why did she? She hadn't completely forgiven him, didn't completely believe in his 'conversion' from hateful, evil menace to society —especially non-white society—to kumbaya good guy.

She didn't believe it because nobody in this cabin was kumbaya. They were all bad guys with no redeeming qualities, working only as toothy dragons guarding society against something worse. Christine was sure she was the only person present who had not killed. It wasn't the Glock that told her the young woman was one of them, it was the wariness. This must be Sergei's wife, the woman who lost a baby last year. She remembered the deference these people had paid to even the government man, Skosh, maybe not as one of them, but as one worthy of respect, the respect of one killer to another. Is that why Paul was admitted? Why Frank smiled? In deference to a fellow killer?

She had not been told what happened to Paul in Montreal, only its aftermath in the forest, but these people knew all about it, judging from Paul's attempt to hide from her his startled reaction to Skosh out on the ramp.

So, did she trust him because they did? No. They didn't fully believe in his change any more than she did. Yet, fundamental change had come to her, after a dismal lack of education, unplanned pregnancy, abusive marriage, and disastrous love affair. She became a police officer, earned a degree, brought up a son she was proud of. She was fundamentally different in every way, except in her determined commitment to nonviolence. Not an easy stance in a law enforcement environment.

So if she could transform from weak, ignorant victim to take executive control of her own business, maybe other changes were possible. Her ex hadn't changed though, despite his life sentence. He was still the very essence of dangerous prison asshole.

But that's him. This is Paul—they are not the same.

Even though many, maybe most, people never change, she had to believe, as if she were an airy fairy Christian saint, that it was possible.

That is why I vouched for him.

34

P aul sensed tension in the man sitting to his left and instinctively wrenched his gaze away from the exquisite blonde woman with the Glock. Speculation sped through his mind. He glanced left, locked onto the colorless eyes beside him, read the warning written there, and carefully lowered his energy. The man on his right gave a low chuckle.

Confirmation. She is defended.

He continued an assessment of the people gathered in plush seats around the empty space in the middle of the cabin. There is a table here, he surmised, checking and deciding it must rise from the floor or else drop from the ceiling. Not deployed, because everybody's hands must be visible. *Check that. MY hands must be visible.* He placed them, palms down on the armrests and contemplated how his presence had dictated furniture arrangement. It made him feel alive, that his presence was acknowledged, even tolerated—for the moment. He was under no delusion.

Christine sat across from Paul between two men who appeared to be father and son. The father had interrogated him quietly last year. The son pulled him out of the dust that soaked up the blood of the man—a former ally—that Paul had just killed. Then there was the tall, lanky guy he met a few months back, and across from him, Frank and the government man, Skosh. Other assigned names that Frank helpfully provided were Mack for the father-type, Charlie for junior here, Mara for the woman he dare not look at,

Sergei on his left whose proprietary interest had been clear, and good-looking Steve to his right. The young long-legged spider who had been with Mack those months ago went by the name Rimas.

Together, they were Charlemagne.

In contrast to Christine-the-cop, Charlemagne was uninterested in evidence, but heavily invested in something they called verification. Bring them *zdat*, Sergei said with an accent, and they would be happy to manufacture plenty of evidence for her.

"Spoken like the old Soviet spook you are," said Steve. "The Cold War's over, Sergei."

The Russian leaned forward to fix his colorless eyes past Paul and onto his friend. "It is not over, Steve. I have told you many times. Habits formed over centuries do not disappear because a government pretends to be peaceful. Okhrana, Cheka, NKVD, KGB, FSB, GRU—all the same. All the time."

"Is it necessary to finish your investigation, Christine?" asked Mara. "Can't you just quietly close it and move on? We can neutralize the guilty man in other ways."

Her voice was so sweet and melodic, Paul did not react at first, but the word 'neutralize' sparked a shiver that became his cue. Christine sat, mouth open but wordless, and Paul came to her rescue. "We have to prove it publicly," he said. "Because of Joe."

All attention, some of it polite, most of it unwelcome, focused on him. The blue-eyed father and son duo became even more still, and Paul, remembering Montreal, took it rightly as a warning sign. He ventured an explanation. "Joe Stinson is our first agent, the foundation of our network, and he's a double."

"Why does that matter?" asked Rimas. "If he is not the murderer?"

"The cops want him to be."

"But they also will need evidence. If, as you say, he is not guilty, there will be none."

"They will eliminate other possibilities and focus on him," said Christine. "He lived in the house and he owned the murder weapon."

"And they will create evidence!" said Sergei, grinning at Steve.

Charlie broke in, eyes steady on Paul. "What do you mean, double?"

Paul described Joe, his jeopardy because of this murder, and his double recruitment as a promising agent.

"And who is this not-Canadian recruiter from Canada?" It was the older one, Mack, who asked. Or prompted. The man already knew the answer, just like he knew all the questions. The same as he did when Paul met him last year in a squalid motel room. *An alternate lifetime ago.*

Paul shrugged in an attempt to dislodge the discomfort. "Last year in Montreal, I met him. My boss at the time was working for him. I recognized him in the coffee shop the day he recruited Joe. I don't think he saw me. He goes by...."

"Rusty."

Confirmation.

"It appears there is more than one good reason for Christine to be victorious," said Sergei. "We must create evidence...."

"Find evidence, Sergei," corrected Mara.

"When we make it, there will be no trouble to find it."

The smug finality of his statement sparked no outcry, no reaction at all, apart from Christine's scowl.

35

T he first thing Christine did back at the office was make a pot of coffee. Out of habit. As a comfort. To counteract the relaxation caused by Charlie's single malt toast with the whole team. The last thing she needed now was to relax. He had been very clear about that. Go forth and find (make) evidence, was the unspoken instruction. So you can get on with your real work.

"I don't get why Fluffy can't look at Frank without showing his teeth," said Paul. "I mean, sure the guy is an old school spook of advanced years—I get that—but why does the dog hate him? Should *we* be trusting Frank?"

Is he learning to trust the dog? Will he ever apply that to me?

She caught and squashed the internal whine. He was, indeed, consulting her, looking for her answer. It was progress of a sort, and as new to her as it must be to him. She poured the first cup for him.

"Yes," she said, handing it to him. "Frank saved my life. I trust him." She ignored memories of all the times she didn't.

"*I* saved your life," Paul said after the first sip, his gaze steady, a bit flinty.

Christine briefly considered if the look held a challenge, but no, he was working from a memory based on incomplete information. Same as Fluffy, who remembered Frank's animosity, not Sergei's swift act of locking the annoying pooch in the attic. She only knew this because she had helped Rimas bandage the Russian's bitten hand.

Funny how the aftermath of her own trauma sharpened that memory—the unimportant one—while at the same time it muddled so much that might be vital.

Paul called her away from insightful contemplation. "So how do cops *find* evidence?"

"Usually criminals just hand it over." She took her first sip. She'd waited too long, lost in useless reverie. It was tepid, almost cold. She poured out the cup in the sink and refilled it, then drank right away, relishing its heat.

He stared open-mouthed, still requiring an answer.

She shrugged. "You ask a criminal if you can search and they say yes. The only thing they like better than that is to confess. So you ask for that, too. Sometimes, you don't even have to ask. At very least, you can get them talking and then sift through the lies."

"You think Greene will go for that?"

"Of course not. He's too scared and too savvy."

Paul took a thoughtful pull on his coffee mug. "No point in searching him. Whatever it is that would hurt him, he's still looking for it. We have the letter his late ex sent to Caslander saying her husband caught an STD in a Thai brothel. If that's what Greene wanted to find, I'm not sure why. And why do we care what's in it? Doesn't it mean she was having an affair with Caslander? Would Greene kill a guy because of an affair thirty years ago? And with a wife he later divorced and maybe killed?"

These were good questions. Christine sat with her elbows on the desk, cradling her cup before her lips, tilting the rim to sip, reviewing these and her own questions.

"Paul," she said tentatively, "you were stationed there around that time."

"In country, yeah, but not at Udorn, where they were. I was at Ubon, in the south, working the Ho Chi Minh trail. Why?"

"Were there brothels, like in the letter?"

He paused to suppress a smile. "Anywhere there's a military base far enough away from the shooting, there will be brothels, Christine. Any kind of military, from any country. It's a law."

"Really?"

He rolled his eyes. "Of nature. A law of nature. There's something about being shot at that sparks a taste for living."

"Greene's wife said he spent all his time there—while she was working...."

"And presumably while she was fooling around with Caslander."

"Then, too. All his time, she said. So, when did he work? What kind of work would he be doing that would allow it?"

Paul's turn to shrug. "Maybe she exaggerated."

"She said he was a worthless layabout and was spending her money on whores. *Her* money, meaning what she earned as a secretary."

"So?"

"So, if he was working, why was she supporting his, um, habit, and also, what kind of job lets him have all that time to spend his wife's salary in a brothel?"

"He was a dependent husband. It sounds wrong because at a military base, it's usually the guy who is the sponsor, but I presume Mrs. Greene's position at Air America included housing and the right to bring family. We know they never had kids, so what else would he do with his time?"

"And what was Caslander doing?"

Paul took a deep breath—of satisfaction? It surprised Christine that she really needed his information. He also seemed to realize he had become important, and it was a shock to him. For a long fraction of a second, they regarded each other as their team coalesced from disparate atoms into a working molecule. Fluffy picked up his head, sniffed the air, and tucked his nose back under a front paw to resume his snooze.

"Caslander was bonking Greene's wife in between missions that won him secret awards," Paul said.

"For what?"

"Mostly for courage under fire."

"Come on, Paul, Justin told us about the awards. I need you to make me understand it—the place, the time, the smells, the sounds. Give me Caslander then and there."

Paul's breathing changed, deeper, then faster. He stared into a corner, winced, scowled and, maintaining the scowl and biting a lower lip, glanced in her direction without meeting her eyes. He was reliving it. She hoped without damage this time.

"Those Air America guys had their own paramilitary groups, Christine, and they ran them against the NVA and VC just like the regulars, only nastier—sometimes—because of the intel angle. So they dropped food and other necessities like weapons and advisors, did reconnaissance, supported strikes, insurgent and assassination operations, extracted bad guys...."

"Extracted?"

"Brought 'em out for interrogation."

"I see. But one of the awards had a few words about life-saving service."

Paul nodded. "These guys evacked the wounded and kept a lot of people out of the Hanoi Hilton when they were shot down. He probably did that more than a few times. He spent six years in theater."

Christine unplugged the coffee pot.

"What are you doing?" Paul showed her his empty cup.

"No time, Paul. We need to find that guy Kerrick, the city council president, and ask him what, exactly, he thinks his mayor, the great hero, did in Southeast Asia."

"I'm with you. I predict it'll track with Caslander's record."

Fluffy leapt from the chair before she got to her keys and began a shrill crescendo of excitement in anticipation of a car ride.

Paul had to raise his voice to be heard. "Where should we start looking for him?"

"Let's try the airport?" Christine shouted back.

...

As her Jeep rounded the end of the runway, blue, red, and yellow lights on ambulance, maintenance truck, fire truck, and police cruisers—multiple— made her stop and ask a gathering crowd. Don Kerrick's body was obstructing the runway, they told her, too dead to answer their questions.

36

"Our boy Greene appears to have only one go-to move for any problem—arrange a death," said Paul. Fluffy snored in his lap.

Christine put the car in gear and moved up one car length in line. The donut shop was extra busy. It was lunchtime. "The cops bought his story," she said, spilling more incredulity into the air. "He convinced them it was an accident!"

"He is their mayor."

Fluffy woke up and sat up. Paul automatically adjusted that front foot to keep the weight off the more tender parts of his lap. Fluffy's ears moved forward, and he panted. He was familiar with this drive-thru.

"What now, Christine?," Paul continued. "I'm thinking it would be good to cancel this guy's future. I mean, for the sake of humanity."

She rewarded him with a withering look. "You're supposed to stop thinking that way, Paul. Remember?"

"Maybe your boyfriend can take care of it for us. I'm pretty sure he thinks that way. And he's an excellent shot."

"What boyfriend?" Her brow was furrowed in honest bewilderment.

That felt good. *So, at least she doesn't call him her boyfriend.* "I could read the sly little half smiles you exchanged with Mr. Daddy Long Legs on the airplane. Don't you think he's a little young for you?"

She turned on a sardonic smile as she said, "Tell me, Paul. If a woman his age were agreeable to you, would you consider her too young? Would you turn her down?" She turned away to move the car up in line, missing his wince.

Confirmation. But he had to give her this small victory. "Touché," he murmured. He took no joy in having been right. "What's his name again?"

"Who?"

"Daddy Long Legs. DLL for short."

She placed their order with the disembodied voice under the menu. Fluffy drooled.

As the car rolled forward, she answered, "He goes by Rimas, which I think is his real name, but I've never heard a last name. And before you ask, he's from Lithuania."

They were approaching Fluffy's favorite magic hunting window. His tail set up a breeze.

Before Paul could get the next question out of his mouth, Christine answered it. "It's a country on the Baltic Sea between Latvia and Poland, next to a tiny, strategic slice of Russia."

"What made you think I was going to ask that?"

"Weren't you?"

Let it go, she won't answer the whole question. It was a trait Christine shared with the people she considered friends when she wasn't calling them criminals. Of course they were criminals. So was Paul. *But now, we're all on the side of the good guys. Right?*

"I'm just not used to the way those guys left so many things unsaid," he said, "but still got right to the point. You do it, too. How?"

She put two large coffees in the cup holders on the console and handed him a white bag full of fast food. Paul lifted it high to keep Fluffy's nose out of it, while Christine pulled over into a parking spot. She took the bag, distributed the over-salted food—Fluffy received a french fry—and took a bite of her sandwich.

"You really don't know?"

Paul shook his head. His mouth was full.

"You're really good at knowing how Joe thinks," she said, "because you remember what it was like to be a twenty-two year old American man. So do that—with everybody. Be that person. Stop thinking that because they look different or talk different or dress different, they don't feel the way you do. Everybody wants the same things. Obstacles are different, but motivations are pretty standard. We're all capable of bad choices, but everybody owns both stupidity and wisdom in all shades of color. *Be* both yourself and that person at the same time. It's called empathy."

Paul watched Fluffy's eyes follow his sandwich as he raised it to his mouth and took a bite. He gave him another french fry from the bag. The dog swallowed it whole. Didn't even chew.

"See? Just like that. If you can do it with a dog, you can do it with people. We're all the same animal. I knew what you wanted to ask next, because it was what I would want to know if I was uncomfortable about Rimas."

"You're not? I saw the guy put a bullet into the forehead of somebody standing next to me."

"That's not why you don't like him."

"Okay. Quit this shit and tell me what I'm feeling, oh wise woman of Native heritage."

"It has nothing to do with my or anybody else's heritage. Get off it, Paul. Quit trying to fit people into boxes. You're pissed because Rimas and I had an affair. You're even more pissed about it because you know damn well you shouldn't be."

Will I ever be able to read minds like that? He gave Fluffy another fry and changed the excruciating subject. "So which of three murders can we pin on our boy, the Dishonorable Mayor?"

37

Fluffy picked his head up when Christine pressed a button on the Justin apparatus. He woke because he had been dreaming about a chase. In a forest. Clicks did not belong. His guardian sensors activated, and he first checked on The Beloved.

She sat at her desk, looking at the talking machine. The Paul had taken over the easy chair. Fluffy didn't mind the theft. Both client chairs were comfortable enough and had the advantage of being closer to Christine. Also, Fluffy had decided The Paul was an ally.

"Frank," Christine said.

Frank was not ally. Allies do not lock you in the attic. Fluffy had a forgiving nature like most dogs, but some things can never be forgiven. He bared his teeth. The voice filled the room. Everybody heard it. He jumped and whirled and searched all corners, but could not find The Frank. Also, there was no smell. How could this be?

"Fluffy, quiet down or I'll put you in the stairwell." The Paul's voice was gruff, like a growl. *He must be angry with The Frank, too.* Fluffy raised the volume until Christine picked him up and sat down again with him in her lap.

Comfort made him quiet. Security allowed him to sniff the air. He felt no tension, no fear, no danger, and no Frank. But there was that voice again!

"What can I do for you, my dear?" said The Frank.

Fluffy listened to the sounds, understanding only voices and a few repeated noises, but feeling the calm in the room. Calm always came with the smell of coffee. Tired also scented the air. The humans should nap, he thought. It was too good a suggestion not to follow it. He tucked his nose under his front leg in preparation, only to take it out again at the sound of Christine's voice.

"Justin said you've gone over the forensic files on the Caslander murder. We're dangling by our fingernails over a chasm, Frank. We need something—anything—that might form the basis of evidence."

The Paul threw his voice across the room: "You know, like maybe satellite photos of Greene walking into that house on the day of."

Christine rolled her eyes upward.

"I won't say a picture doesn't exist somewhere," said The Frank, "but if it does, we're not likely to have access. What we do have is unknown blood at the scene, according to the report. It has DNA."

They said it together. "Whose?"

"That is the mystery. It's not hers—Mary Catherine's, I mean. They took a sample from her that day. Ditto her son when they had him in custody. It's not his, either."

"Then he should be in the clear," said The Paul.

Christine shook her head. "No. The science is still too new. They like having him in their sights. They'll gnaw that bone until somebody throws them a better one."

Fluffy understood 'bone' and wagged the tip of his tail in anticipation.

The Paul shook his head. "You don't know that."

"I do know it. I was a cop, remember?"

"Then start throwing them bones, my dear," said the machine on her desk.

Fluffy momentarily reassessed his opinion of The Frank and waited, but a bone did not appear. Resentment returned.

The voice continued, "Maybe you could get a sample of Greene's DNA."

"We could have Joe do it," said The Paul. "It would be great training—a real world operation for him to cut his teeth on."

Christine tilted her head and shook it just a little. It meant no. "No," she said. "It would be hard to do in an admissible way. We'd need chain of custody and Joe would have to be able to testify in court, which would blow his cover."

A new voice came over The Justin Apparatus. A voice from before and a voice from just before, when they met those people on the airplane, most of them with familiar scents. One of them was speaking.

"Christine, you only need to convince Greene that you have the evidence. I will help you."

"Thanks, Rimas, but I'd rather…."

"I insist."

"Has he been listening the whole time?" murmured The Paul, scowling.

"Are you even in the country?" asked Christine.

"I can be. We should discuss it on the secure phone."

Fluffy was aware of new tension, but not from Christine. She hung up the call with a relieved sigh. The Paul snorted and deepened his scowl. Next, he would likely snarl. Fluffy prepared himself.

38

When loneliness hits a man like an infection without remedy, a sensation never experienced, an ache in all the parts of him he thought were in perfect health: memory, will, desires, and ambition, it becomes time to examine the pathogen, trace its origin, evaluate the severity, and render a prognosis.

Paul did not have the vocabulary, experience, or introspection to deal with this new pathology. He had always been solo. He worked for his cause and considered himself an obedient part of the Christian Identity movement, but his every act was isolated and deniable. His bosses told him what they wanted and left it to him to make it happen—alone.

Those bosses—the ones who now wanted him dead— were out of his life and for that he was grateful. The new ones represented by Frank had the same ruthlessness and menace. Maybe they took greater care of meeting his most basic survival needs, and they certainly displayed a strange reluctance to cause collateral damage—a thing the previous regime considered a plus, a propaganda tool to twist into the other side's fault.

But the solo nature of Paul's life had not changed.

So what the fuck is eating at me?

He slipped a long tool into the ridiculously easy lock on the hangar's side door. The door led to the open space, away from the office. He squeezed inside, adjusting his eyes from moonlight to deep gloom. The small flashlight he carried would not show him much—yet. He concentrated on finding the right airplane. It should be easy, but these machines were hangared for repairs, with cowlings off and parts missing, and they were all of a size—light aircraft. He knew nothing about aviation beyond the noise and terror of the gunship he had fired a cannon from, thirty years before.

The object of his search squatted in the front, just inside the hangar doors. *Logical.* The incident happened this morning. The cops were done with it. They had dismissed Greene's fingerprints on the right-hand door as unremarkable. He owned the aircraft after all. *Also logical.*

Moonlight seeped through the cracks between the large doors, making him once again appreciate Christine's thinking. At least, he hoped it was hers and didn't come from....

The airplane's right side door hung by one crosspoint screw on a welded lower hinge. The latch had failed, said the police. And as Kerrick fell through the door during a steep bank, camera in hand to photograph the airfield below, his body twisted the hinges, with one giving way entirely. The seat belt was off, Greene had told them, because he needed to hang his upper body from the window for the shot.

The police dutifully took fingerprints, found both men's prints on the latch, declared mechanical failure due to wear and tear and deemed it accidental death.

"Check the hinges," Christine told Paul earlier. She gave him a tiny camera that looked like a pen. "Get pictures."

She answered a phone call just before he left and did not put it on speaker phone. She also didn't say hello into the phone or mention the name Frank.

She's meeting Daddy Long Legs. Why the fuck does it bother me?

Paul got the hang of the little camera. He found a way to hold it and snap the photos in quick succession. Even low light would be sufficient, she told him, but he took extra time to take at least one shot of each door part holding both flashlight and camera.

The door latch could have failed due to age or lack of maintenance. There were no indications of tampering, and the aging airframe showed normal wear. The top hinge, though, was missing its cotter pin. He searched the floor for it without result and could not imagine how it might have worked loose without falling inside the cabin.

The other hinge had a permanent, non-removable (and non-removed) pin joined to a welded plate bearing two screws into the door. One screw still held. The other was broken at the back of the welded plate. The plate itself showed signs of what Paul could only think of as unwelding. The join to the frame had felt the heat of a blowtorch—recently, considering its shiny patina.

Before going in search of the blow torch, Paul took one of the touch DNA kits from his vest pocket, swabbed, secured, and labeled the sample. He did the same with the blowtorch, which he found on its side at the back of a work bench littered with engine parts and tools.

It won't do any good, he thought as he jogged across the tarmac in the brief darkness provided by a cloud floating across the face of the moon. Not that reliable. No chain of custody. *Yadda yadda.* He knew this collection was part of a larger plan—a plan proposed by Rimas, AKA Daddy Long Legs, the DLL in Paul's lexicon, with his youth and his East European accent, which gave him way too much credibility with women, and… *so what if she slept with him?*

Sleeps with him, he corrected himself. *Is that why I'm pissed?* This whole introspection thing was new to him.

With only a year of experience in examining his motives and emotions, Paul had a habit of taking it easy on himself when it came to his stand on other people. Having abandoned white supremacy, he figured he made the most important change and now it was a matter of tweaking the occasional racist habits, like reacting badly to things like skin color.

Am I jealous?

He delved deep. Yes, he would sleep with her if he could. No, he didn't want that, because there was something more he needed, something he only recently acquired. He knew the whole plan and his part in it. She told him before sending him to the hangar. That level of confidence never happened before. His solitary, secret life was over.

It was better than sex. *Wait a minute, nothing's better than sex.* He amended that first thought. This was not better, it was *more* than sex. It was a condition of mutual trust in an occupation marked by universal distrust. Paul had become a kind of Fluffy, zealous in his self-appointed role as fierce guardian and completely dependent at the same time. He didn't want to lose it.

And he sure as hell didn't want Daddy Long Legs disrupting it. The team—their team—was still too fragile.

39

J oe sat at his mom's kitchen table putting together the spice rack he'd bought for her. Guilt nagged. He pushed it away. His career had begun; it was what he wanted; and he had a strategy.

"You should come home, Joseph," she pleaded. "I can't do without you. You haven't even read the directions and look at you building the rack for me." She glanced at the directions on the table. "I can't understand a word of this." She looked again. "There aren't any words! Only pictures. It's impossible. Every day there is something like this. I need you here."

The last sentence was an order, and Joe was grateful for it. He had begun to weaken—until the order stiffened his spine.

"Ma, I'm right here, and I'll keep coming around when you need me. I'm still in the county, ten minutes away. It's not like I moved out of the state." *Yet—or the country—yet.*

Rusty's 'friend' from Portland brought more education to Joe than anything else that happened so far this semester. She stayed in one of the nicer Bangor hotels and took him to a restaurant he'd never heard of, with a valet to park her BMW and wine with dinner. The waiter didn't even card him. The wine relaxed him enough and her cleavage enticed him sufficiently to take up her offer in her hotel room.

Joe had always been curious.

"You can't know that," Mom had said, way back in middle school. "It's this smut society, Joe. They put ideas in your head. When you grow up, nature will take its course and those thoughts will go away."

He'd spent high school waiting for those thoughts to go away. Instead, during junior year, his friendship with Jason, a senior, blossomed into something more. It wasn't just the sex. It was the tenderness Joe missed when Jason went to an out-of-state college on a basketball scholarship.

Shortly after Joe's graduation, Jason broke his heart in a *Dear Joe* email. Mom had no solace to give, only disgust and a renewed effort to keep him home, safe from satanic influences. Depressed and defeated, he scrapped his plans to join Jason out of state.

He scrapped all plans to go anywhere. Until he met Paul. Joe knew instinctively that Rusty would not be any more sympathetic than Mom was, but would Paul? Especially now that Joe had tried a woman, courtesy of Rusty? He was grateful for the experience. It was very positive, indeed, but it taught him more about his own reality.

Should I tell Paul?

Paul's emphasis on teamwork and integrity made it advisable. But the man was pretty old school, and Joe was not up for disappointment in a man he had come to admire.

What about Paul's boss, Christine?

He remembered their brief interview in her car the day he got out of jail. She was an Indian, like his mother, but less sweet. Analytical, maybe, and definitely the boss. If Joe's nature didn't fit the work, she'd know. And she'd handle it without Joe having to lose Paul's regard. She had at least that much mom in her. She'd care about that.

40

O n the one hand, Paul was delighted with Christine's progress. There is no greater compliment for a teacher than having a student who excels after only one lesson. On the other, it's an awfully painful compliment when it involves throwing the instructor onto the mat with force.

And then she chose that moment to ask a difficult question.

"How do you feel about Joe?"

Feel? At the moment he felt the need to breathe. He wanted to see where this was going. Paul could only see the barn rafters above him as he sucked air to replace what she had knocked out of him—by using one of the throws he just taught her.

"What do you mean?" he gasped.

"You told me once that you left Christian Identity because you realized non-white people have souls. That's how you put it. They have souls. So do you see a soul in Joe?"

Shit. It was better with Joe than it had been, sure. At first, Paul could only see the ponytail and high cheekbones —much like Christine's.

But hers are different.

He didn't see anything in Joe's eyes, like he had in Christine's. Then Joe had rolled those eyes upward in repressed rebellion when Paul rebuked him for not checking his surroundings carefully before servicing a dead drop. This universal indicator of late-adolescent scorn brought the memory of twenty-year-old Paul doing the same. His eyes had pretty much lived in the rolled up state when he was a kid.

So, he saw a me-ness in the young man, and the slant of his eyes became familiar, and the faith the young man had in him called for reciprocity beyond the requirements of the job. But Paul had to out-process almost five decades of indoctrination and lack of contact with anyone not exactly like him. He was working on it. He could say, now, that he liked the kid. Could he tell her that? Would she give him time for all the rest? Could he ever see everyone beyond their differences like he did with her that day in Montreal?

She was waiting for an answer.

Paul came to a stand slowly, used his towel to wipe the sweat, stalling for extra time while his brain worked the word problem. "Yes, Christine. I see the same soul in him that I had when I was his age."

She raised one side of her mouth in a crooked smile. "When you were his age, you were a white supremacist. You have the tattoos to prove it. Do they have souls?"

"You're goading me. Why?"

"I'm sorry. I need a new level of truth here, Paul. Tell me about your twenty-year-old soul and about his. I really need to know, and I'll tell you why as soon as I do." She picked up his water bottle and handed it to him. "I promise."

He let a long gulp give him time to form the answer.

"I'm not sure what you need, but my soul, if that's what it was, pretty much mirrored my family, especially my granddad. He was a good man up to a point and that end point was the walls around the church compound he built for our pastor. Outside was bad; inside was good. When I was ten, my mother opened the gate and walked down the mountain, alone, just the clothes she was wearing, a kind of billowy long blue dress.

"I watched for her a long time. I watched for buzzards, too, but I never heard her name mentioned again. Granddad took up the slack—kind of. I went to live with him, because my dad was joining the active wing of the movement. Granddad taught me honor and loyalty, hard work and righteousness, fear and loathing, suspicion and how to shoot.

"At sixteen, I was pretty much done with the religion bit. I don't remember exactly which passage it was— something about being nice to the stranger—but the pastor's answer was... well, let's just say it was bullshit and I knew it. But I was already in training to be a warrior for my people and there were perks with that."

He looked away at the memory of the girls who were coming of age. He'd have first pick, they said. Problem was, he was on the road so much doing God's vengeance on unbelievers, that they were all married before he got back. Not the first lie he had believed, nor the last. He looked into those deep brown eyes of hers.

"So, by Joe's age, I was an unformed puppy and a killer who took orders. Those were the only two things I was good at. Your turn."

"Remember Montreal?"

He snorted. "You're not serious. It changed everything."

"You weren't in that open air theater...."

"Correct, I was outside killing the guy trying to kill you."

"I heard about that. I'm glad you won, but while you were busy in that fight, I was in charge of protecting the guy everybody came to see, who is a hero to us. I do not carry...."

"We should talk about the wisdom of that in this business...."

She grimaced. "The others on the detail were from various tribes in New England and Canada and they all carried, so there was no need for me to be armed. One was a Penobscot from Old Town, a little older than Joe, named Eric. Somehow, somebody turned him. He betrayed us and was deployed by an enemy to shoot our hero. Mack took care of it, quietly, right there in front of me. I want to know both the who and the how that turned Eric. That's why I agreed to set up this network for Charlemagne."

"What does it have to do with Joe?"

"The only thing I've found out so far is that Eric had a dysfunctional family. So does Joe. It's a different dysfunction, not as vicious, but smothering is another way of killing a spirit, you know. Joe needs to learn his trade and he needs enough skill to protect himself, but I hope he's not a gung-ho tough guy like Eric was. Is he?"

Paul shook his head. Where was she going with this? "If you're worried he'll turn, Christine, I don't see any sign of it. He likes me. He doesn't like Rusty."

"Then your influence is paramount. I know some of your background, Paul. Do you like Joe unconditionally enough to not let your instincts interfere with this project?"

He wrinkled one side of his nose in a questioning half-sneer. "Spill it, Christine."

She took a deep breath, engaged him eye-to-eye and said, "He's gay."

Paul stepped backward, banging his heel on a leg of the bench behind. Sharp pain in his foot complemented the confusion in his mind and created focus. A year of internal crisis and the struggle to resolve it, to change, to process his new way of being, had not prepared him for this. The kid gave no sign.

Wait.

After reviewing their brief history, Paul admitted to himself he noticed an underlying gentleness in Joe. He had found it endearing. Was that just Joe, or was it...? After another internal examination, he suspected it didn't matter.

He briefly closed his eyes and took a breath. "I won't lie, Christine. It's a shock, and he's the first one that I've met in person...."

"That you know of," she said with a wry smile.

He paused to unclench his teeth and nod. "That I know of. I accept that everybody is capable of everything and how you're decorated doesn't affect what's inside. I get that. But this is more than a decoration." He looked away from her scowling face before continuing. "Then again, it occurred to me recently—in another context—that it's none of my fucking business what other people do behind closed doors, so long as nobody's being hurt or forced."

When he met her eyes again, her smile dazzled him.

...

Paul knew that, unlike Christine, who could do a workout like this and still look fresh, he smelled a little rank when the Mercedes pulled up outside the barn. When he helped her into the front passenger seat, the driver with the long eyelashes and Texas drawl pointed him to the back. He climbed in next to the impeccable DLL. *He's way too young for you, Christine.*

The younger man wrinkled his nose.

Why can't I unclench my jaw?

41

C hristine held Fluffy in her lap as they pulled away from the barn, leaving Paul's truck around back. Of course they took the black Mercedes SUV the Charlemagne team preferred. The driver, Steve Donovan, was one of the criminals she met in Montreal the previous year, the way-too handsome one with dreamy brown eyes and long lashes. The excessively alert skepticism in those eyes and set of his jaw brought back memories that increased her caution.

Paul sat next to Rimas in the back, probably chewing the same poisonous arguments he spit and sputtered last night.

He spoke. "I thought you guys always traveled with the whole pack. How come there's only two of you?"

There was no answer. The question did not deserve one, Christine knew, and so did Paul. He was being over-nosey because he wanted to start something. She dropped her chin and sighed. The air was still too full of argument. They carried it into the car with them—two major doses of it in her office between last evening and this morning. She was sick of it.

She closed her eyes and concentrated on the time between the spikes. The memory slowed her breathing and brought a smile. She dropped it back to a scowl when she noticed Steve's glance.

Paul had been a pain in the ass about these two guys staying with her in her one-bedroom apartment upstairs. Of course he knew better than to say so, but she could feel it in everything he said. He did not like Rimas.

For her part, Christine could only appreciate her young lover. Especially since his skill in that department had only increased since Montreal. There was no future with him, but she appreciated the *now* he brought her. Why Paul couldn't see that...?

He had left in a huff to complete his assignment at the airport. Steve slept on the couch. Rimas did not.

She smiled again.

"I still think it's a lousy plan, Christine," said Paul. "The man's a killer for chrissake."

The irony took her breath away.

Steve did a half nod. Rimas said, "I agree."

It was the only thing that united these three. This hard-won argument ended in the adoption of her plan, and none of them took it with grace. "Let's not go over all of it again," she said. "Just the part about evidence being admissible in court. Not one of you thugs can get on a witness stand."

"It would be simpler for me to shoot him," said Rimas. "Or, Steve can break his neck."

"So can Paul, for that matter. Again, the point is to convince the cops it wasn't Joe so they'll leave him alone."

"They'll have trouble pinning it on a mayor, Christine," said Steve. "They won't want to go to trial, anyway. One of us should do this. The guy's fucking dangerous."

This was again too rich for words, but she thought them anyway, then let go of them immediately. She didn't know Steve well enough to provoke him without risk. The only chance she was willing to take this morning was meeting Greene at the coffee shop on Broadway, about a minute away.

Steve drove past it on the left.

"What are you doing?" Was he doing that protective male thing, the *I know what's best for you, little lady?* She let her exasperation show.

"Relax," came the Texas drawl. "Greene shouldn't see you get out of the passenger side of this car." He turned left into the neighboring fast-food parking lot and stopped out of sight of the coffee shop. "Walk from here. I'll pull in and park before you get to the door."

"Nobody's coming in with me. We agreed."

"Fine. Go."

She turned in her seat and hoisted Fluffy over the console to the back, handing him to Paul. Fluffy yelped and resisted, scrambling his legs in the air to come back to her. Paul took hold of him with a questioning look.

"He'll be safer with you," she said. The look turned into confusion. Two thirds of her team would still be intact—if anything happened.

Nothing is going to happen.

She repeated the mantra internally as she walked up to the corner table where Greene held his habitual audience with sycophants and hangers-on, his hands cupped around a cheap ceramic mug on the table. Christine was gratified to see it needed a refill.

Now to business.

"Hello, Mr. Greene. Do you remember me?"

He sucked his teeth and gave an arrogant tilt to his head. "No. Can't say I do." He swung both hands, thumbs out, and with a pointed look told the other three men at the table to scram.

In the next moment she was alone with him. He said, "What the fuck do you want, bitch? I should have had you arrested at the airport that day."

I want that mug in your hand. She was careful not to look at it. "Please let me apologize for that incident, Mr. Mayor," she said, stretching her lips into an uncharacteristic smile. "I'm new to the area and had no idea who you were. I was looking for a Mr. Caslander to interview him for a feature article about the

Vietnam War, but I understand he died recently. Is that correct?"

"Yes." The man's scowl softened, but the brow was still lowered with suspicion.

"I wanted to speak to you, sir, because I just found out you were also decorated during the Vietnam War. You see, I am a freelance journalist. I'm writing a feature on local heroes. Several people have told me you worked for Air America."

He tossed his head, chin up, and gave a minimal nod.

"Then you did work for Air America," she said, maybe a little too loudly. "Somebody said you even got a medal that is even more rare than the Medal of Honor. Let me see...." She pulled a flip notebook and a pen from her purse, opened to a page, and looked up at him. "It's called Distinguished Intelligence Cross. They say it's usually posthumous!"

She hoped she wasn't overdoing the look of infatuated wonder she had pasted on her face.

Greene smiled, glancing to one side, then the other, eyebrows mobile with pride. "Yes." He was playing it cool.

Christine suppressed a chuckle.

"Can you tell me about it, Mr. Mayor?" She opened her eyes wide, beseeching, dripping admiration. It made her stomach turn.

"No, I'm sorry, my dear. It's classified."

She forced a look of disappointment. The interview was going swimmingly. Still, the hardest part was yet to come, she reminded herself. The thought helped her quash the smile of triumph that threatened.

"The reason I wanted to talk to Mr. Caslander was because I know he was awarded the Intelligence Star." This was a deliberate lie. Christine noticed a momentary surprise in Green's expression. "But yours is above that, isn't it? From my research...."

She pretended to search the scribbles in her notebook, still talking fast, "He flew helicopter rescue missions in combat and everybody says you did, too. I've heard some of it, but I could use so much more, at least the unclassified bits, straight from the source. Would you be willing? Can I refill your coffee so we can talk?

She swooped up the cup as he nodded, strode to the counter and put the cup in her purse.

Phase one, complete.

42

F luffy was not entirely comfortable, and it wasn't a simple case of The Paul's less than padded lap. It was the atmosphere, the static air, full of electricity but empty of movement beyond the rise and fall of ribcages in these men. He elected not to curl up. It was difficult to see anything from his precarious perch on Paul's knee. The car had moved after Christine got out, but Fluffy rightly surmised they were watching the place where she must have gone, and he added his special powers of observation to the effort. It did not matter that The Paul's scent was heavy. In the tense stillness of the car, Fluffy could discern every pheromone left behind by The Beloved. He was also used to the smell of their weapons, of the cleaning agents and oils and leather holsters. He brought his own weapons to this watch: teeth and claws and voice.

"I really don't like this," said The Paul. Fluffy did not turn to look behind him, but he heard the sound of a scowl. In his experience, scowls were dangerous contortions of the human face. It raised his vigilance.

"Why does she refuse the transmitter?" asked the tall man next to them in the back. "I can respect her misguided decision to remain unarmed, but we should be able to know if she is in trouble."

"She doesn't want anything to taint admissibility," said The Paul. "No third parties. She's convinced the man is powerful and hard to pin down." He was silent for several breaths of time, then said, "But I agree with you," with his word noises squeezed between his teeth.

Fluffy could tell The Paul did not like the tall man Christine called Rimas. Though Christine liked him, Rimas stole Fluffy's cuddle time, so he was not a favored human. But if Paul was in accord with him, it edged Rimas further into the friend category. Humans were peculiar. Maybe Paul did not mean serious animosity. Fluffy could feel a general tightening of the muscles under him and a change in breathing.

The man in front spoke. "Rimas, Christine is all about the US Constitution and this here thing we call The Rule of Law." Fluffy heard the capitals in this speech, though he was unacquainted with grammar. "Once upon a time, I believed it, too. Pledged to defend it, give my life for it, in fact, until they tried to take me up on that. So, that's why she's taking a fucking unacceptable risk in there. She's about to confront a killer in public, hoping for a reaction. And we don't even know if he's armed, but we know she's not."

"Of course the man is armed, Steve," said Rimas. "He is American."

All the muscles in Paul's body were adding to his strong smell. The thighs beneath Fluffy were becoming stone.

The man in front spoke again. "So whaddaya say we do what they might call an intervention?"

Fluffy turned his head to see what it looked like when a human turned entirely to stone.

43

She felt the presence to her right as she pretended to scan the menu above the counter, steeling herself and stalling for time. Christine glanced down at the feet next to hers. Italian shoes, sharply creased and expensive wool trousers. She narrowed her eyes and forced a whisper through her teeth. "Why the hell are you in here?"

"Modification to the plan," came the even softer whisper in a Texas drawl. He drained the cup in his hand and put it on the counter next to him.

Laughter in male voices rose from the table where she left Greene. His friends were returning and the situation was developing exactly the way she wanted it. But now this gargoyle loomed over the scene.

"What modification? Who says?"

"We decided you need back up."

"We?"

"Me and Rimas."

"What about Paul?

"He said you're in charge.... What? Did you beat him into submission or something? Sexy...!"

She gave him the look he deserved. "Why isn't he stopping you?" She gave herself an interior kick. Paul would be no match for these two and a dust up would really derail her plan. Point to Paul for strategic inaction.

Donovan read her thoughts, confirming them with a half-smile. "Where's the mug?"

"In my purse. I ordered a fresh one."

"Give it to me."

"Like hell."

"Look at them. There's too many. How you gonna get it back if they grab the purse?"

She glanced at Greene and his three friends at his table as she took a full coffee mug from the top of the display case. She saw four aging, pot-bellied grizzlies. *They wouldn't dare!* Surely she could handle it, especially with the methods Paul had taught her. All she needed was Greene to make the attempt, right? The attempt and the blurt, the guilty words in front of witnesses, in front of his own friends.

"Look at me, Christine," said Donovan, *sub voce*. She turned slightly and stared past his long lashes, the kind any woman would, and often did, pay money for, into the hard depths of a way-too-intelligent criminal. He spoke again. "You're assuming those guys ain't willing to lie for him."

Fuck. Another hole in a swiss cheese of manufactured provocations. She needed the blurt, the attack, Greene's allies turning on him—anything that would unhinge him and make the police take notice of the evidence. But there had to be witnesses.

She whispered, doing her best not to look like she was talking to Donovan. "His DNA is in blood found in Mary Catherine's house. How will he explain it?"

"He won't have to. It's too new and he's too well connected."

Leave it to a criminal to understand the justice system better than she did.

"Fine. Here." She turned so that the purse was between them, against his arm.

"Okay," he murmured.

How does he do that? She had felt nothing. "Now get out of here."

"No, and stop fuming. I'll stay out of your little show, but I will see you safely out the door, whatever happens. It was the one thing all three of us could agree on. Do you want my empty mug as a decoy? If you get the reaction you want, they might be satisfied with just taking it off you."

She dipped her chin ever so slightly. This time, she felt the extra weight land in her purse.

"Now go," he said, "see if you can cause a scene. Get yourself an Oscar."

By now, the fresh cuppa was sufficiently cool that it did not burn her fingers when a few drops splashed out as she approached the table. Christine brought up her most cheerful smile, aware it made her look foolish. Counting on it. She placed it before Bobby Greene as the table became silent. She did not sit down.

"Here you are, Mister Mayor. And it's in a clean mug." She patted her purse. "I took the liberty of keeping the one with your DNA in it. We'll see if it matches the sample from the crime scene where Lew Caslander was murdered."

I'm rather proud of that. No stutters. No extra drama.

And no reaction. Her spirits fell. Then, Bobby Greene lost it.

"You bitch! I'll fuck you up so bad death will be a relief. Hand it over right now."

He was out of his seat; his friends were standing; he was rounding the table toward her.

Christine maintained her old cop stance, casual like Andy of Mayberry but ready like Bruce Lee, as still as a ninja. She felt the satisfaction of being both right and ready, but had no time to bask in it. They were on their way. Though time slowed in this emergency, it was not infinite. She heard her voice address the three others also approaching her.

"You heard him, gentlemen. He just admitted to murder."

"We didn't hear nothing, lady," said one as he wrenched her purse away from her by the shoulder strap.

It came away easily because she was busy putting her elbow in his buddy's eye, then practicing the new take-down Paul showed her on number three. By now, Greene had come around the table and had both hands heading for her throat. She blessed the day Paul insisted she strengthen her kicks. The Mayor went down clutching his pain and she headed for the door, noting there were more people in the room than these guys. *Some of them must have heard it.*

The guy with her purse was as yet unhurt. Somebody yelled to him to get the license plate of her car. She was out of his range, but she worried that the damned Mercedes was distinctive and momentarily considered running in a different direction.

Steve Donovan moved to intercept the guy behind her, flashing a hand signal to keep going. She made it through the door, heard the tussle behind her, and headed through the lot to the Mercedes. Rimas was at the wheel. As Christine climbed in the back next to Paul, Steve took the front passenger seat almost simultaneously.

"That compromised you, Steve," she said. "And I didn't need any help."

"He didn't see you get in the car," came the slow drawl from the front. "He was busy. I apologized for stumbling into him. He was picking up the wad of bills he used to have in his pocket. He didn't see me get in the car either." Steve reached over the back and handed her a wallet. "I left him patting all his pockets."

Christine took the wallet with reluctant respect for skilled criminals.

44

Joe went to the meeting because Paul told him to. His mother needed him there, Paul said. It was time he got to know more of the tribe, especially the elders.

And don't let on that you know Christine when you see her.

That was all. Nothing about why, what it was about, or who else would be there.

Get used to it, was the answer.

It wasn't the certainty of a more punishing workout with Paul if he didn't go that made him acquiesce, though that did sit at the back of his mind. Both Paul and Christine had been indoctrinating him about loyalty and faithfulness. So had Rusty. The difference was Rusty was sly about it. The other two came across completely upfront with what they were teaching him. He knew he was free to walk away at this stage. With Rusty, even though the man never said anything directly, Joe could heard the subtle threats in his conversation every once in a while. So he helped his mom into a chair across from Christine at the tribal office conference table and sat down next to her. Each chair had a dark blue folder in front of it on the table.

"You look so good in a suit, Joseph," his mom whispered, "but you should cut your hair. It makes you look effeminate."

"It's tradition, Ma. In a lot of cultures. In ours, too."

"It just doesn't go with the suit, Joseph. Businessmen cut their hair."

George James's could not have been better dressed or his entrance better timed. The flawless crease in his trousers, the perfect fit of his jacket across wide shoulders, tie straight and subdued created the image of success and authority, amplified by the simple beaded black band containing the ponytail reaching half way down his back. He came in with the sheriff and sat down at the head of the table, with Mary Catherine on his right, Christine on his left. The sheriff took a chair at the other end, on the left of the federal attorney general. An FBI investigator sat on his right.

Mary Catherine glowered and looked away.

Others entered and took the remaining seats, some from the sheriff and attorney general offices, others from the tribe. George nodded at Christine, and she began by opening her folder and taking out the first document.

"This is an obituary of Lewis Caslander, the victim. I think every loss of a life to murder is a tragedy and wanted to give you all a sense of what the world has lost in Mr. Caslander." She looked from George to Sheriff Johnson and to the AG, pausing at the deputies and staffers between them. "I will be submitting this obit to various publications and hope you will help with that. Please, take a moment to look it over."

Joe read it, took a deep breath, and risked eye contact with Christine for a moment as the others finished. He hoped she understood the intensity of his stare, the fervor in his eyes. *I'm all in, Christine. I'm on the right side. Your side, Paul's side, and especially Lew's side.*

Others were reacting. There were murmurs as people shifted in their chairs.

"How does this help us, Christine?" said George.

She held up a hand in a private signal for patience.

"Where the hell did you get this information?" asked the federal investigator.

"Wait," said one of the sheriff's deputies. "This sounds like that guy in Morgan. The politician there. This is *his* record, isn't it?"

A second deputy said, "Yeah, the mayor of Morgan. My brother works for that city. He told me about this guy. Said he's a real hero. Were there two of them?"

Christine maintained eye contact with the sheriff as she said, "Caslander's record was declassified after his death. I have a contact who was able to get me the information."

But the momentary respect in the sheriff's expression faded as Christine took a ceramic mug wrapped in plastic from her carry-all. She handed it across the table to the deputy next to him. "I think you will find the DNA in this mug matches the unidentified DNA found at the scene of Caslander's murder. It has not been out of my possession since I obtained it from the subject. I can testify to chain of custody."

The room filled with murmurs as the sheriff narrowed one eye at her. "Who is it?"

Christine raised her chin and continued, "I can also testify that I obtained this evidence in a public place before many witnesses who will be able to verify the subject's inculpatory reaction." She sat back in her chair, maintaining eye contact. "And finally, I will be happy to testify, if necessary, that no one in this room is implicated by the evidence."

Joe felt the eyes as they swiveled his way, all three officers, puzzled, perhaps disappointed, and most important, George James, with an almost-smile, triumphant.

45

It was the sound of Fluffy scrabbling after prey down below that made Paul roll off his cot in the loft. He rubbed the two-day stubble on his chin and threw on a t-shirt that did not match the pajama pants he wore. There was no mirror available to tell him how bad he looked, for which mercy he was grateful.

Christine stood at the bottom of the ladder, prying a mouse out of Fluffy's jaws. She held the victim by its tail with thumb and forefinger and headed for the old barrel in the corner they used for trash.

"This is full, Paul. Don't you ever empty the garbage?"

Fluffy was busy nosing through a crumpled fast-food bag at her feet, searching for old crumbs and stray french fries. Christine laid the mouse at the top of the pile that filled the barrel.

"Good morning to you, too," he said, resisting an urge to scratch various itches as she turned around to look at him. No need to reinforce her already low opinion of him. *Well, not low, just not as high as I'd like.*

She hit him immediately with the question of the week, of the month, of the year.

"Do you think it was suicide?"

He could stall by pretending he didn't know she was referring to Greene's death the day before. No point. He shrugged, which was the truth. He just didn't know what he thought about it.

"It could have been the full story in the local paper that made him do it," said Christine. She frowned as her voice ended almost in a whisper.

She's feeling guilty. He had to fix that. "No, he could have just left town after the exposure. He was the kind who would do that. I don't think it was suicide." A fib. He just wasn't sure. "Do our friends have a habit of hanging people in their garages?" It was a straw. He offered it for the sake of the other nook in her conscience.

She dropped her eyes and shook her head. "I don't think so. I'm sure Rimas wouldn't, and Steve's specialty is the unfortunate fall down a stairway."

Paul watched her exonerate herself and her lover— *damn him.*

She met his gaze with a half smile. "The rest of the team wasn't even in the country."

How the hell does she know?

"Then it was his own cult followers who arranged it," he said, "when they discovered all the lies. He died the evening of the day the whole story came out in the paper." This theory had the advantage of being plausible enough that he ranked it higher than either suicide or the team. *But we'll never know.*

"The cops are relieved, anyway," said Christine. "The sheriff and local PD made it plain they weren't happy with the evidence I gave the AG, and frankly, I was going to have to avoid mentioning Donovan in my testimony. George is happy, though. So there's that."

"The tribe paid you?" The itch under his arm made him squirm. *Cut to the chase. I need coffee. And a shower.*

It was a relief to hear her change to her business voice. "The tribe paid *us.* Come to the office and clean up. There's enough for a deposit on your own place.

You'll need to find one with a shower. We'll pick up a coffee maker for you after you've signed the lease."

...

Christine always preferred solitude, but was beginning to distrust absences. Paul was gone an entire day during his apartment hunting. That he found one two blocks from hers made it worse. Now, he was too close. Convenient, yes. Comfortable, no.

...

Fluffy noticed only the positive side of this change. His ally, The Paul, was still helping him protect The Beloved most of the time, but he no longer used the waterfall upstairs. Fluffy had always been of the opinion that getting one's fur wet is unhealthy, especially for creatures who cannot efficiently shake out the water.

Now, if only he could convince Christine.

Epilogue

S traight-man's gaydar was useless compared to Joe's. The first time he laid eyes on Dan, he knew. It had nothing to do with the young man's beautiful, almost girly, eyelashes. Dan was around Joe's age and all male in all respects, except the one, the important one. Dan's perception of him was equally spot on, but that time, he hadn't stayed in town long enough for them to get acquainted.

The message came through Christine, thank heaven. Paul was surprisingly okay with Joe's orientation, simultaneously awkward and casual, but Joe had to wonder what would happen if he was pushed with more new realities in his world.

The meeting place was an airplane, and the approach made in accordance with the dictates of tradecraft. It took him time to get to the small jet sitting on the ramp, engines already whistling. Dan sat in the right seat, wearing a headset. The red-haired woman next to him handed Joe her headset as he stooped behind them.

"I didn't want to say anything until I knew it was possible," said Dan turning in his seat. "I'll be back from time to time. Maybe we could have a beer together?"

Joe was too stunned to answer with a resounding yes, and instead spit out a stupid "but procedures?" It was obvious, and not just from Christine's admonition, that these people were in the game, as Paul called it. Would Joe be allowed to mix pleasure with business?

Dan raised one corner of his lips in a half-smile. "Difficult does not mean impossible."

The End

If you enjoyed this book, consider leaving a review at your favorite book store. To get the earliest news about the next Fluffy mystery, sign up for the Charlemagne Files Newsletter at https://www.charlemagnefiles.com/contact.